# Mending Jodie's Heart

## *When Paths Meet Book 1*

## *By Sheila Claydon*

Digital ISBN 978-1-77145-073-7

Amazon Print ISBN 978-1-77299-820-7

Books We Love
A quality publisher of genre fiction.
Airdrie Alberta

# Dedication

For The Red Stripe Band which unwittingly triggered this
story.
Thank you for the music

# *Acknowledgments*

It is important to get it right when dealing with such
sensitive topics as Autism. If I have managed to do this
then it is entirely thanks to Lesley Fleming who is
passionate about the potential of people with autism and
who works tirelessly to make it happen. She read the
manuscript of this book several times and her comments
and suggestions were invaluable. Through her, Luke came
alive. My thanks also to the Riding for the Disabled
volunteers who let me watch them at work and, just as
importantly, allowed me to make a fuss of their wonderful
horses.

# Chapter One

"You can't do that!"

"Watch me," the man in the yellow fluorescent jacket barely glanced at Jodie as he snapped the heavy padlock shut, closing off access to the bridleway.

Reining in Buckmaster to steady him, she tried to explain. "But you're not allowed to close it. It's a public footpath as well as a bridleway, and...."

He interrupted her with a shrug. "I don't make the rules Miss. I just do what I'm paid to do. You got a problem with that, then talk to the boss."

"I would if I knew who he was," she could feel her temper beginning to flare.

The man jerked a thumb over his shoulder as he started to walk away. "Him what's having the house built."

Jodie looked in the direction he'd indicated. There was nothing there except a dense tangle of undergrowth and a copse of windblown pines. With an exclamation of annoyance, she wheeled Buckmaster around only to find the workman had disappeared.

"Now what do we do?" she asked the large chestnut gelding who was waiting patiently for his morning gallop. He twitched one ear at the sound of her voice and then skittered sideways as a flurry of leaves blew around his ankles.

She kicked her feet out of the stirrups, slid to the ground, and looped his reins over the gatepost. "Don't worry gorgeous boy. You'll still have your ride. I just need to do something first."

In less than a minute she had climbed over the gate onto a sandy path and forced her way past brambles and weeds to where a derelict building crouched under a gloomy canopy of misshapen trees. With a hiss of pain as a rogue plume of gorse scratched her hand, she retrieved her riding crop from where it had become entangled in a bush, straightened up, and stared at the old farmhouse. It stared right back, its boarded-up windows giving it an air of blank disregard for whatever fate was awaiting it. And fate certainly had plans if the scaffolding piled against the walls was anything to go by.

Picking her way through a scatter of fallen roof tiles, she walked across to where old trees creaked and moaned above fast encroaching undergrowth. It was dark and gloomy and smelled of damp and decay. There was nothing else though. No notices on the door announcing its imminent destruction. No labels on the scaffolding. Not even a phone number she could call.

As she turned to go back to Buckmaster a splash of color caught her eye. Blue paint. The tree nearest to her was circled with a band of blue paint about a meter from the ground. She walked a little further into the wood. There was another one. And another. She lost count before she reached twenty. A lot of trees were going to be felled, but for what?

\* \* \*

Buckmaster gave a welcoming snort when she re-emerged shaking burrs and a couple of small insects from her clothes. She started talking as she walked towards him.

"We've work to do Bucky. Someone has bought the old farmhouse and we need to find out who it is. I don't care what happens to the house, or to the woodland, and neither would you if you could see it. It's far too spooky for you. You'd do your prancing about, rolling your eyes thing if I took you in there. I do care about the bridleway though. That's why we have to find out who's bought it, and go visit them. We need to tell them they can't lock us out."

She had clambered over the gate while she was speaking and now she rubbed the white blaze on his forehead. He pushed his nose against her shoulder and blew gently into her ear. She laughed as she seized his reins and with a cursory touch to the stirrup, leapt onto his back.

"I knew you'd see it my way. Now let's find another route to the beach. You've waited quite long enough."

As she guided Buckmaster around and then paused to check for traffic, a tall man, muffled up in a thick padded jacket and wearing a wool beanie on his head, climbed down from a parked 4 x 4 and walked towards her.

"What's going on here?" he asked with a frown.

"Someone's bought the old farmhouse," Jodie told him. Then, noticing he had a dog sitting in the back of his car, she shook her head.

"You can't walk your dog down the path anymore. Nobody can. Whoever owns it seems to think it's okay to close the bridleway, but don't worry, I intend to find out exactly who it is. I'll make sure it's opened up again even if I have to chain myself to the gate."

Kicking her legs against Buckmaster's flanks, she trotted off down the lane without waiting for an answer.

The man stared after her in irritation. He didn't seem to have handled that very well. When he'd asked the girl what was going on he had expected some sort of lame excuse; an embarrassed explanation as to why she was clambering back into the lane over a locked gate. Instead she'd been angry and said something about organizing a protest. Then she'd ridden off without a backward glance. He gave an inward groan. A stroppy teenager threatening to stir up the locals. Just what he needed. He was going to have to get some *No Trespassing* signs put up as soon as he could.

He walked back to his car and lifted down a very old dog, making sure it had full control of all four paws before he let go.

"Come on Blue. Time to see your new home."

The dog, a dusty looking black Labrador, wagged its tail, and then waited patiently while its master searched in his pocket for the key to unlock the gate. Then it followed him along the roughly cleared path that Jodie, in her impatience, had missed, until they could both see the house.

# Chapter Two

"Haven't any of you heard anything?"

Jodie was sitting at the old wooden table that was the focal point for everyone who worked at the riding school; the place where they left messages for one another, dumped their belongings, or grabbed a mug of coffee when they had a moment to spare. Jodie was drinking coffee now; or rather she was stirring her coffee round and round while she addressed the people in the room in general, and the girl sitting next to her in particular.

"Nothing! Nix! Nada! I already told you," Carol shook her head in exasperation. "For goodness sake Jodie, don't get so worked up about it. I'm sure it's just a misunderstanding."

"Misunderstanding!" Jodie's voice went up several notches. "How can anyone misunderstand a bridleway? And it's a public footpath too don't forget. Understanding that both of them have to be kept open is hardly rocket science."

"I guess...but it's still not worth getting into a state about something that can probably be put right by a call to the local council."

"You reckon?" Jodie didn't share her assistant manager's faith in authority. It had let her down too often in the past.

"Yes! And I'll prove it to you," Carol reached behind her to where some local telephone directories were stacked on the windowsill, selected the one she wanted, and began to rifle through the pages. A moment later she was punching a series of numbers into her cell phone.

Jodie listened to the ensuing conversation without hope

and when, after several minutes, Carol finally cut the call, she gave a resigned shrug.

"Told you."

"The man I spoke to said they were aware of it," Carol protested.

'He didn't say they were going to do anything about it though, did he?"

"No. Apparently it's not an official bridleway, or a footpath for that matter. He says the new owner is quite within his legal rights to close it."

"Even though everyone who lives around here has been using it for years?"

"Yes. The family who used to own the land didn't care who used it but apparently the new owner does. The man at the council said he values his privacy or something like that."

"Well guess what? I value my bridleway, and so should you...all of you. So what are we going to do about it?" Her eyes were fierce as she looked around the room.

Before anyone could answer her the door swung open and smacked against the wall with a thud. Five heads swiveled, and then five pairs of eyes opened wide as a gawky teenager wearing a spectacularly ugly school uniform fell into the room.

"Izzie!"

"Sorry folks. Not at all the entrance I was aiming for." The girl picked herself up with a grin and untangled her feet from the heavy school bag that had tripped her.

Kicking it under the nearest chair she seized Jodie's mug, swallowed a mouthful of coffee, and helped herself to two oatmeal cookies from a tin that was open on the table. Then, spraying crumbs, she said the one thing destined to gain the attention of everyone in the room.

"Did you know that Marcus Lewis is moving to the village?"

It was several minutes before Jodie could make herself heard over the excited buzz in the room. When she finally did, everyone stared at her in disbelief.

"Who is Marcus Lewis?" she asked.

Coughing over a crumb that had gone down the wrong way, Izzie rolled her eyes and shook her head speechlessly, leaving Carol to answer.

"Don't tell me you've never heard of him," she pleaded. "He's a jazz pianist, or at least he used to be. You must remember him. In his heyday he won every award going. I don't know why he stopped performing but he's still a huge part of the music scene. He's written stuff for everyone and he's composed some fantastic film scores too."

Jodie shook her head. "I've never even heard his name before."

Then a new thought struck her and she swung back to where Izzie was sitting on the edge of the table, still red in the face from her coughing fit.

"Where is he going to live...this Marcus Lewis?"

"I think he's bought the old farmhouse down by the beach."

Jodie seized her arm. "Who told you?"

Izzie stared at her, surprised by her vehemence. "Someone at school. Her Dad's an estate agent or something. Why are you so bothered when you don't even have the first clue who he is?"

"Because your Marcus Lewis is the man who has closed the bridleway."

"My Marcus Lewis...I wish," Izzie grinned as she shook her head in puzzlement. Then she looked around the room.

"Is anyone going to tell me what's going on, and why my dear sister seems to have gone ever so slightly mad?"

* * *

Jodie's temper wasn't any better by the end of the evening. For a start she and Izzie had spent so long trying to track down Marcus Lewis' contact details on the Internet that she knew she wasn't going to get her paperwork finished unless she stayed up until long after midnight. To make matters worse they hadn't been able to find out anything useful. No phone number. No address. Just a website full of musical stuff. Izzie had scrolled right through it but Jodie had given up and pushed back her chair in disgust. It wasn't what she wanted.

"Lots of celebrities try to stay under the radar," Izzie had soothed, stretching her back when she eventually got up from where she had been hunched in front of the computer. "If they made it easy for fans to find out where they lived…well it would make their lives impossible."

"It doesn't help us though, does it?" Jodie grumbled.

"No, but we can send an email to his agent's contact address. We did find that. And anyway he's bound to turn up in the village eventually. You'll be able to talk to him then."

"Not if he's such a celebrity I won't. He'll probably travel everywhere by limousine, with minders or something."

"Whatever." Izzie gave a wide yawn and rubbed her eyes. She'd had enough of Marcus Lewis until he actually moved into the village. When that happened she was going to do everything in her power to get to know him, but when she spoke to him she wasn't going to waste time talking about bridleways or footpaths. Not that she was about to tell Jodie that.

# Chapter Three

The tall man in the wool beanie was leaning on the top bar of the gate on the third morning Jodie rode by. He was gazing into the straggle of woodland while a very old black Labrador sat patiently beside him. The man in the yellow fluorescent jacket, the man who had secured the padlock in the first place, was just getting into a van that was idling at the curb. With a twitch of the reins she pulled Buckmaster to a halt as he drove away.

"What did he tell you?" she demanded.

The man in the beanie hat swung around and stared up at her, a look of puzzlement on his face. He had very blue eyes.

"What do you mean?"

"Did he say how long it would be before they start building? Did he say how long it will be before Mr. Marcus…I can do exactly as I like because I have a lot of money and this is my land…Lewis, turns up? No he didn't, did he? I can see from the look on your face that you've no idea what's going on. I bet he didn't even tell you when they're going to start cutting down the trees."

Without giving him time to answer, she slid down from Buckmaster's back and walked across to the gate to stand beside him. Her head barely reached his shoulder. Together they surveyed the tangle of undergrowth, and then Jodie turned towards him, her body taut with impatience.

"Didn't he tell you anything?"

"Not about the bridleway, no," Marcus Lewis shook his head. He was torn between irritation, amusement, and just a little admiration. She was certainly passionate about

12

her damned bridleway that was for sure. Courageous too. He could still remember what she had said about chaining herself to the gatepost.

"Why is this bridleway so important anyway?" he asked. "There must be others."

"There are," she conceded, looking up at him. "But we have to negotiate a lot of traffic to get to them. This is the only one that takes us straight down to the beach."

"We?"

"The children who use my riding school."

"You work in a riding school?"

She nodded dispiritedly. "For what it's worth I'm the manager, so I've a vested interest in keeping my riders safe."

His gaze slid over her. It didn't compute. She wasn't much more than a teenager. As if she knew what he was thinking she suddenly grinned at him. It totally transformed her face, changing her expression from angry to something altogether different. He found himself responding with a smile of his own as he wondered if the hair hidden under her riding hat was as dark as her eyes.

"I'm older than I look," she told him as she took hold of the horse's saddle and vaulted onto its back. "Way, way older. Plenty old enough to give Marcus Lewis a piece of my mind when he eventually turns up. In the meantime, I'm going to start gathering protest signatures."

"I thought you said you were going to chain yourself to the gate," he said, squinting up at her against the early morning sun.

She laughed as she began to move away, pleased he had remembered. "Don't worry. I'll be doing that too, but not until the journalists arrive. I want to inflict maximum damage to his reputation."

* * *

He watched her go. She was a good rider. She sat straight and true in the saddle, moving rhythmically, guiding the horse beneath her with only an occasional

13

twitch of the reins. She was attractive too, despite the riding hat and the shapeless green fleece that hid any curves she might have. Good looking, courageous, passionate…a girl worth knowing in different circumstances. Then he shrugged and turned back to the gate. Those No Trespassing notices were still going up. After all he had Luke to think about.

# Chapter Four

It was three weeks before there was any more action. Then a flat bed truck turned up and off-loaded a shiny new trailer. Jodie saw it arrive when she passed by on her daily reconnaissance. The tall man with the dog was there again as well. He was standing beside the open gate, apparently quite unconcerned that he was in the way. Jodie waved to him but she didn't stop because she didn't want the bustle and the noise to spook Buckmaster.

By the time they returned from their morning gallop along the beach, all was quiet. The tall man was still there though, only now he was contemplating a large red notice board that had been erected on the other side of the gate. Jodie stared at it.

THIS IS PRIVATE LAND. ALL TRESPASSERS WILL BE PROSECUTED

From her position, sitting high up in the saddle, she could see that a second board had been erected at the far end of the bridleway as well.

"It's war now," she said. "There's obviously no point in appealing to his better nature. Those signs prove he hasn't got one."

"He is entitled you know. After all it is his land." Marcus Lewis walked across to where Buckmaster was blowing through his nostrils.

"And I thought you were on my side," she said in disgust. Then she wheeled about and trotted away, her parting words floating back to him on the breeze. "If you

15

want to sign the protest there will be a list for signatures in the village shop."

He watched her go. He didn't know why he hadn't told her who he was when they first met, or why he was compounding the problem now. After all she was bound to find out sooner or later because it was very clear she wasn't going away any time soon. He sighed as he bent down and patted his dog.

"I guess I'm a coward Blue," he told him. "But at least I know what I'm up against now. A protest campaign that's being run by the village shop!"

\* \* \*

Marcus underestimated the power of the village shop, however. Within a few days Jodie's campaign had garnered a lot of sympathy, and once people from outside the village started adding their signatures to the list, the local Press got involved.

At first it was just a couple of lines telling readers about the protest. Then it was a half page picture of the closed off bridleway with the No Trespass sign featuring prominently in the foreground. By the third week things were a lot worse. Marcus, who had been away on business and so had missed the earlier papers, stared at the lurid headline in barely contained fury.

ACCIDENTS INEVITABLE AS MUSIC MOGUL FORCES RIDERS ONTO THE ROADS

Underneath was a picture of that dratted girl and her horse. The caption said she was called Jodie Eriksson, and she was flanked by a group of small children. Marcus knew publicity when he saw it, and he could see they had all been told to look as miserable as possible. If he hadn't been so angry he would have found it amusing.

He grabbed his cell phone and called his agent. He needed to organize some damage limitation as soon as possible.

* * *

The following week he was standing on the steps of the trailer talking to his site manager when he saw Jodie clamber over the gate and start to walk up the path. She was clutching a folded newspaper in her hand and from her furious expression he knew he was in trouble. Deciding he had better meet it head on, he excused himself and strode towards her.

"You do know you are trespassing," he said.

She glared at him. "Did you enjoy making a fool of me? Did it amuse you to pretend to sympathize and then go away and laugh about me with all your celebrity friends?"

Wondering what she would think of him if she knew he could count his celebrity friends on two thumbs, he shook his head.

"I haven't discussed you with anyone. I didn't set out to deceive you either...I...it just never seemed to be the right time to come clean."

"Huh!"

One word, but somehow she managed to make it radiate disbelief and contempt. Her eyes were the same. They might be dark brown and luminous and set under finely arched brows but they were hard and unforgiving.

He knew a sensible person would just point to the No Trespassers sign and send her on her way but suddenly, and inexplicably, he found himself minding very much what she thought of him.

"Come into the trailer. Join me for a coffee while I try to explain things."

"What's to explain? You made your feelings very clear in your newspaper interview. You have no intention of opening up the bridleway. Your personal privacy is far too important."

"Maybe. But I didn't say why."

"You didn't need to. Your picture says it all. It's obvious you want silence so you can be ready when the muse strikes."

17

She thrust the newspaper at him as she finished speaking. It was folded open at his picture and he cringed inwardly when he saw the PR shot his publicist had chosen. It was the one where his hair was slightly too long and slightly too artfully arranged, where his silk shirt was open one button too many, and where his pose was soulful and serious. In it, he looked every inch the poseur maestro, right down to the white grand piano behind him. No wonder she thought she knew why he had refused to open up the bridleway.

He shook his head again. "It has nothing to do with my music. It's because of my son."

"Your son? The article doesn't mention you have a son."

"That's because I don't talk to the Press about him."

"But you're talking to me."

"Yes I am, because I want you to understand why I can't open up the bridleway however much you want me to. I want you to understand why Luke has to be protected."

Her expression didn't change but at least she was listening. He took a deep breath.

"He has...a learning disability."

"And?"

His temper flared. She was impossible. "And nothing. Isn't that enough for you."

"No. Not unless you think he's about to be kidnapped or something."

"Now you're being ridiculous."

"I don't think so. Explain to me why his learning disability affects the bridleway?"

"Well for a start he's frightened of people. A new face can make him hysterical for hours. He's the same with people he does know if they turn up unexpectedly. He finds a lot of things challenging and that's why I have no choice but to keep the bridleway closed...I need to protect him from himself."

"So you're going to turn your home into a fortress without any regard for the local people you're going to

18

upset in the process. Tell me, do you really think that is what your son needs, or is it just the easy way out?"

Surprised she was still challenging him, he met her gaze and saw something close to sympathy had crept into her eyes. He resisted it. He wasn't interested in sympathy. He just wanted her to understand about Luke.

She gave the tiniest of smiles when she saw his scowl. "Maybe I will have that coffee after all, but only if I can bring Buckmaster inside the gate."

Now it was his turn to give the ghost of a smile. "Don't you ever go anywhere without that damned horse?"

\* \* \*

Five minutes later Marcus led the way into the trailer. Buckmaster, now tethered to the branch of a tree, watched them go. Then he resumed his hopeful search for a few blades of grass amongst the builder's rubble and the piles of old flagstones.

Jodie looked around the trailer with interest. It was the sort of thing she imagined movie stars used on film sets except it was being used as a site office. There was a desk immediately inside the door. It was piled high with architect's drawings, and there was a laptop computer too. It was open and working, its cursor winking impatiently at the end of a half written sentence.

Marcus led her beyond the desk to where the trailer opened up into a comfortable sitting area. He gestured to the black leather couch that took up half the space. His dog was stretched out on a rug in front of it. Jodie bent down and patted him.

"Make yourself comfortable while I brew some coffee."

"Don't bother just for me. Instant will be fine. It's all we ever have at work," she told him as she sank into the cushions.

He grimaced with distaste as he moved across to the kitchen area. Then he grinned. "I guess only liking fresh coffee makes me seem like a spoilt rotten celebrity too."

"Just a bit," she nodded with the trace of a smile. "But I'm prepared to be persuaded it's all a big mistake and you're a just regular guy who is misunderstood."

He ignored the sarcasm and concentrated on the coffee. When it was ready he offered her sugar and cream before settling himself into a corner of the couch.

"I'm not you know."

"Not what?"

"I'm not a spoilt celebrity. I mostly live a very ordinary life and I do everything I can to avoid the limelight."

"For you, or for your son?"

He sighed. "For both of us I guess. It was bad enough when his mother died but he was only a baby then, so it didn't hurt him. Now he's older any Press intrusion sparks a hysterical reaction that sometimes lasts for days. That's why I have to protect him."

"Where is he now?"

"At our home in London."

He sat forward and watched the steam rising from his cup as he tried to explain. He was finding it difficult because he never discussed Luke with anyone. He wasn't even sure why he was discussing him with this irritating girl, or why he cared what she thought of him.

"Luke is autistic. He goes into total melt down over things that don't bother most people at all. The only way to keep it to a minimum is to maintain a routine. If he knows what's going to happen every minute of the day he stays relatively calm, so I employ a team of people to care for him. They follow a set program 24/7. He does schoolwork, he exercises, he draws and paints, but all at exactly the same time every day. Although I've tried, I haven't been able to find any other way to help him. I have to make sure he's pre-warned before visitors arrive too, especially if they are people he doesn't know, so the thought of an open bridleway full of dog walkers and horse riders doesn't bear thinking about. He would be in permanent melt down if I kept it open, surely you can see that."

Jodie heard the pain in his voice and understood how

20

much effort it had taken to talk to her, so her voice was soft when she replied.

"I'm sorry about your son.  Truly I am.  And I do I understand. But hasn't it occurred to you there might be another way?"

She didn't flinch when his head jerked up. Instead she kept her eyes steady. "I know you think I'm talking out of turn and maybe you're right...but I do know about challenging behaviors because I run a program for disabled riders. You'd be amazed at the miracles the horses achieve. Even just coming along to watch might help your son get used to being around new people."

Marcus gave a short, hard laugh that was devoid of any trace of humor. "And you think this would succeed where everything else has failed I suppose?"

"I didn't say that.  But once he's settled into his new home wouldn't it be worth giving it a try? If nothing else it would give him a chance to experience something different, something that might teach him to cope outside of that routine you've set up."

Swallowing the last of his coffee he stood up, irritation written all over his face.  "You don't know Luke.  He wouldn't even pat a horse let alone ride one, so thanks, but no thanks.  Now if you'll excuse me, I've work to do."

Jodie stood up too. "Okay. Have it your way, but maybe you should ask me why I want the bridleway kept open so badly.  It isn't for me; it's for children just like your son; children with problems who come to ride our horses but who need to be kept safe. So just remember that when you can't sleep at night Marcus Lewis."

He clenched his fists as he watched her jump down from the trailer. Then he turned back to the coffee machine and refilled his mug. She could see herself out.

# Chapter Five

Jodie was very quiet when she returned to the riding school. Everyone noticed but nobody said anything. They knew better than to enquire about her feelings. Jodie's personal life was a closed book. Nobody ever got near her except Izzie. And Izzie didn't talk either. All anybody knew about the sisters was that their parents had died when Izzie was small and that Jodie took care of her.

Only Carol, who was the nearest thing Jodie had to an intimate friend, had ever been inside the cottage where they lived, and whenever she stepped over the threshold she was always shocked by how bare it was. No pictures on the walls, no family photographs, and a TV that looked as if it had seen better days in someone else's house. The few pieces of essential furniture were obviously second hand too, and the drapes at the windows were thin and tired looking. The bookcase was stuffed full of books, however, and bizarrely, there was what looked like a brand new, up-to-the-minute computer on the kitchen table.

She glanced across the tack room to where Jodie was pulling towels from the dryer and wondered, for the umpteenth time, why Izzie attended the most prestigious private school in the area when it was clear they had barely two pennies to rub together.

She had never seen Jodie in anything other than her riding gear either. Nor did she wear makeup, or do anything with her hair. Not that she needed to she thought enviously as she pushed her fingers through her own frizzy curls, because her friend had hair to die for. If she had hair like that then she certainly wouldn't wear it in one long plait day in and day out, the way Jodie did.

As if she sensed she was being watched, Jodie straightened up, swung around and looked straight at her.

"What?"

"Nothing…that is…is something the matter?  You've hardly said a word since you got back from…"

"My coffee break with Marcus Lewis…the unexpected meeting of minds that has all of you sniggering behind my back you mean."

"That's not true," Carol flushed slightly as she shook her head.

Unexpectedly, Jodie grinned at her.  "Yes, it is, and according to Izzie it's all my own fault.  Apparently I am the only twenty-eight-year-old in the whole world who wouldn't recognize him at ten paces."

"Perhaps it's why he talked to you.  Perhaps he likes being anonymous…you know…the way some celebrities say they do."

Jodie shook her head decisively.  "No, it wasn't that. He just had something he wanted to say but he didn't know how to say it, so he invited me in for coffee to buy himself time."

"What, Marcus Lewis?  You must be joking," Izzie picked up the tail end of the conversation as she stepped into the tack room trailing her school bag behind her. "He's used to performing to a whole arena full of people and he gives Master Classes to students. How can someone like that struggle with words?"

"I don't know.  I'm just saying how it was.  And will you please pick up your bag before it gets covered with mud and straw."

Izzie hoisted her bag up onto her shoulder with a long-suffering sigh.  "So what was it he had such trouble talking about then?"

Jodie shrugged.  "Just some personal stuff."

"And…?"

"And nothing.  It's not important."

"Jodie! Any personal conversation with Marcus Lewis is important. He's the man who has shaped the musical

23

tastes of a whole generation: your generation as it happens. He has probably just told you something the local paper would love to know about and yet you don't think it's important. How come, when this morning you were ready to tear him limb from limb? What has he done to you?"

* * *

Later, washing up their supper things while Izzie finished her homework, Jodie pondered her sister's words. What had Marcus Lewis done to her? What was it about him that had made her reluctant to repeat their conversation? And why had he told her about his son anyway? He had freely admitted he liked to keep his personal life out of the public eye, so why had he taken such a risk? Why had he trusted her when, for all he knew, she might go straight to the Press and blow the whole story.

After sluicing down the sink she upended the dish mop into a pottery mug Izzie had made for her years ago and stared out of the kitchen window. It was dark outside; too dark to see anything but her reflection in the glass. She looked at it for a long minute and then twitched her thick plait over her shoulder and slowly removed the elastic band holding it secure. With a toss of her head she shook her hair free and started to brush it with the hairbrush she had left lying on the windowsill that morning.

She was still brushing it when Izzie came into the kitchen to say goodnight. She gave a sigh of envy as she planted a kiss on Jodie's cheek. "If Marcus Lewis could see you with your hair down he would open up that bridleway in a heartbeat."

Jodie frowned. "Don't be ridiculous...and anyway, when did you become so knowledgeable about men?"

Raking her fingers through the wheat-colored pixie crop covering her own head, Izzie returned her sister's frown. "I'm not exactly a child anymore you know. Besides the girls at school never talk about anything else."

"Well I hope you're not one of them. You're only sixteen. You've another two years of school ahead of you,

24

and then university. You've got better things to do than waste your time giggling about men and worrying about whether they like long hair or not."

"Seventeen, I'm nearly seventeen. I'm almost the same age you were when Mama died, and you didn't think you were too young to take care of me then did you? Seventeen is practically grown up. Besides there's nothing wrong with thinking about men, or even having a date. I can do that and still get an education you know."

When she saw the stricken look in Jodie's eyes she laughed. "Don't worry. I'm not dating, not yet anyway. And when I do, I'll tell you. I'm just saying it wouldn't be the end of the world. Nor would it be the end of the world if you tried a different approach with Marcus Lewis...you know, ride Buckmaster Lady Godiva style, just covered by your hair. That would get his attention!"

Jodie's tart response died on her lips as she stared at her sister's retreating back. What if Izzie was right? What if a softer approach would work? What if she could persuade Marcus Lewis to open up the bridleway by using her feminine wiles?

A single glance in the mirror propped up on the windowsill was enough to put paid to that idea. What feminine wiles? If she had ever had any, she'd lost them, along with her innocence and her belief that the world was there just to do her bidding, the day her stepfather died.

With a sigh she began to plait her hair again. For once the paperwork could go hang. She would do it tomorrow. Right now all she wanted was to go to bed.

* * *

Two hours of tossing and turning later she gave up trying to sleep. Thrusting her feet into her slippers, she pulled on a dressing gown that had once been fleecy and pink but was now fuzzy and beige thanks to years of repeated washing, and made her way downstairs. If she couldn't sleep then she may as well do the paperwork after all.

25

She fired up the computer while she waited for the kettle to boil. Maybe a hot drink and an hour or so of staring at the riding school's accounts would do it.

She started off full of good intentions. Tapping in figures with one hand while she lifted a mug of hot chocolate to her lips with the other, she tried to concentrate. It worked for about ten minutes until her mind strayed back to Marcus Lewis. Damn the man! Why couldn't she get him out of her head?

She gave a sigh of irritation as she keyed his name into the computer's search engine. Maybe if she checked him out she would be able to find a clue about how best to disarm him. If she could make him see how important the bridleway was to the children who attended the disabled riding program, then maybe he would change his mind about closing it. Maybe he would change his mind about his son too.

She clicked the computer mouse and his name flashed up on the screen. There were hundreds of links. Some referred to songs, some to films, and some to newspaper articles. Her hand hovered indecisively. Then she clicked on his website. The website she had once ignored in disgust.

His face stared back at her: thin and serious and as familiar as his dark hair with its frosting of silver, and his blue, blue eyes. She would have known who he was much earlier if only she'd bothered to look over Izzie's shoulder when she was scrolling through his website searching for his non-existent contact details. Irritated with herself, she clicked on the *All About Marcus* tab and began to read.

She didn't stop until she had absorbed every last detail of his professional life including his list of musical compositions, the film scores, the concerts and appearances…it went on and on. Marcus Lewis was obviously a workaholic. Nobody could produce that amount of work and have a private life as well. It just wasn't possible.

She clicked back to the opening page, back to his picture, and stared at it. The pain was right there in his eyes, the pain she'd seen when he told her about his son. The deep down despair was there, too, if you knew what to look for, and the helpless anger. His image misted over as her eyes filled with tears. She could see all of it in his face because she identified with it. Those feelings were the ones she lived with every day of her life.

Closing the computer, she pulled a screwed up tissue from her dressing gown pocket and scrubbed at her eyes. She wasn't going to cry. She never cried. She had cried enough to last a lifetime when Mama died and when, for one terrible year, she had thought she might lose Izzie too, so she wasn't going to feel sorry for Marcus Lewis because she had more than enough problems of her own to deal with.

Tipping the cold remains of her drink into the sink, she trailed back upstairs to where a triangle of light from her sister's bedroom bisected the landing. Pushing the door wide she took four silent steps across to the bed and looked down at her.

She was curled onto her side, her knees drawn up and one hand tucked under her cheek. Lying on the pillow beside her was a threadbare rabbit with one eye. Jodie's hand hovered over her for a long moment until she pulled it back and stuffed it into her pocket. Gone were the days when she could smooth back Izzie's hair and kiss her cheek while she was asleep. As she had told her only a few hours earlier, she was almost grown up. And it was true. It had been a long time since she had crept into Jodie's bed when she couldn't sleep. She was no longer the little girl who needed constant reassurance and the physical contact of hugs and kisses. Those days were gone. And it was good they had. Nowadays she could pass for a normal teenager, and mostly an exceptionally intelligent and level headed one too.

Nowadays there were even moments when Jodie, her life too constrained by work and worry to invest in learning new things, felt younger and less sophisticated than her little sister. It was only when Izzie was asleep that she could see the shadow of the frightened child she had once

27

been. It was there in the open doorway. It hovered over the nightlight. And it made its presence most felt when she fell asleep clutching her cotton rabbit.

Jodie's heart lurched. How was her sister going to cope when it was time for her to go off to university? They were going to have to talk about it…find some sort of solution. Maybe she could choose a university close to home so she could still sleep in her own bed.

# Chapter Six

Marcus glanced up from his computer as the trailer door opened, expecting to see his site manager. Instead, a leggy blonde wearing too much make up and too few clothes confronted him.

"Who the hell are you?" he demanded.

"Nice." she said. "With a few tweaks it would make a good headline."

"So would journalist thrown out for trespassing on private property."

"It would if it were true," she conceded, pushing the trailer door shut behind her and leaning against the wall.

Marcus sighed. A groupie. That was all he needed. He'd spent months searching for the right place to build his house, looking for somewhere close enough to the main arterial roads that led to airports and big cities to make travel easy, but isolated enough to give him the peace and space he needed to concentrate on his work. Isolated enough, too, to protect Luke from the outside world that so distressed him now he was growing older.

The search, the negotiations, the meetings with architects and builders had eaten into the hours he needed to complete his latest project, but he had considered it worth it until the girl with the large chestnut horse had disrupted his plans. And now this. He hadn't even considered fans, and if he had he would have dismissed them, sure they would be few and far between in such a small, tucked away village.

He stood up. "Who let you in?"

"Nobody. I climbed the gate."

"Didn't you see the no trespassing sign?"

"Oh that," she waved a hand as if the red and white board was a mere inconvenience. "I didn't take any notice of it because I knew you'd talk to me."

"Really. I'd be interested to know when you figured that out. Was it as you were climbing over the locked gate, or was it when you walked past the sign?"

She grinned at him and for a brief moment he was pierced by a sense of bewildering familiarity. "It wasn't any of those. It was because you talked to Jodie."

He frowned. "Jodie, as in small, dark and irritating? Jodie as in permanently attached to a large chestnut horse?"

"That's the one," she agreed, her grin stretching wider. "And you're right, she can be very irritating, but it's only because she cares."

"So you're not a fan. You're here about that damned bridleway."

Yes…no…I mean…yes I am a fan, and no I'm not here about the bridleway…well not specifically anyway."

He shook his head. "How about you just tell me what you are here for…specifically…and then you go."

Ignoring his sarcasm, she pushed herself off the wall and stood upright in front of him. As she did so her grin faded and she suddenly looked very serious.

"I want you to give me music lessons."

Whatever he had expected, it wasn't that. For a long moment he stared at her, then he burst into genuine laughter. She had nerve, he had to give her that. And if she was aiming at a stage career then she had the right equipment too. Tall and willowy with legs that went on forever, she looked good.

His laughter died when he noticed the desperation in her eyes. She wasn't anywhere near as confident as she looked. Underneath the provocative clothes and the makeup, she was frightened to death, but there was a hunger there he recognized from his own past. Against his better judgment the musician in him was intrigued.

"You're not joking are you?"

She shook her head and for a moment he thought he

30

saw the glitter of tears.

"So tell me what you have in mind. Am I supposed to give you a singing lesson or a piano lesson, or maybe you just want to learn to write music. What is it you think I can do for you that all those people who teach music for a living can't?"

She leaned forward, her fingers white with tension as they pressed against the desk.

"Lessons not lesson," she corrected him. "And it's none of those things. I want you to teach me stage techniques. I want you to teach me how to perform."

"And I should do this because…?"

"Because I have an amazing voice. And because I want to make it as a singer."

"So why not take the time honored route and start touting for gigs in pubs and clubs? Or maybe you feel that every day the world doesn't hear your amazing voice is a day wasted."

She didn't even hear the sarcasm this time. Instead she leaned even closer; close enough for him to see he had been right about the tears.

"I'd start searching out gigs tomorrow if Jodie would let me, but she won't. She wants me to go to university and study something noble like medicine or law. And I know I'm clever enough to, but it's not what I want. I want to leave school and take my chances as a singer, and once you've seen how good I am you'll know I'm right, and then between us we might just be able to persuade her."

"Whoa!" Marcus backed away until the chair behind him forced him to sit down again. "Before we go any further would you mind telling me exactly how old you are?"

She shook her head impatiently. "What's my age got to do with anything?"

"A lot when you're shut in a trailer with a stranger. How old are you?"

"Sixteen…so you don't need to worry because I'm legal. Actually I'm almost seventeen," she added, her eyes flashing defiantly.

He groaned. "If you think being sixteen gets you off the hook then you've a lot to learn about life young lady. Besides it's not just you I'm thinking about, it's my reputation as well."

"Oh you don't need to worry about that. I didn't tell anyone I was coming to see you. Jodie thinks I'm at home studying."

"What about your parents?"

"They don't think anything. They're both dead. There's only Jodie. She's my sister. If it wasn't for her I would be in care or adopted or something. I owe her everything and I'll do absolutely anything for her except give up my dream of making it as a singer. That's why I need you to help me. I need you to persuade her I'm good enough to try."

He shook his head. "I don't know what has given you that idea but you couldn't be more wrong. Your sister wouldn't listen to me if I were the last man on earth."

"She would. I know she would. She's been moping around ever since she had coffee with you, and Jodie has never moped about anyone before."

He gave a wry smile. "I think you'll find her moping has nothing to do with me and everything to do with the bridleway."

"No it hasn't. If it was just about the bridleway, then she'd still be mad. But she's not. She's just…well, mopey. Everyone has noticed it. And when I asked her what the two of you talked about, she snapped my head off."

Marcus stared at her wordlessly. He had been waiting for a phone call from the local paper ever since he told Jodie about Luke, which is why he had thought this girl was a journalist when he first saw her. Yet here she was, telling him Jodie had never breathed a word of their conversation, that the protective silence he had built around his son hadn't been breached.

Still not sure what had prompted him to open up to Jodie in the first place, and irritated by the number of sleepless nights he had suffered because of it, he was surprised into an overwhelming feeling of relief. This was

32

quickly followed by an unwelcome sense of obligation.

He pushed back his chair, stood up again and, stripping off his sweater, thrust it at her. "Against my better judgment I'll give you thirty minutes, but before I do I'm going to brew some coffee. And while I do that, you are going to put this on, open the door and sit on the step in full view of passersby. I don't want anyone wondering what's going on inside this trailer.

Her grin came back as she took the sweater from him. It lit up her face, banishing the glitter of tears and putting a smile into her striking turquoise eyes. "No chance of that," she said. "There are no passersby. You put up a No Trespassers notice, remember?"

For a fleeting moment he saw the resemblance again. The smile was Jodie's, even though they were physically very different.

"You don't look anything like your sister," he said, ignoring her jibe.

"Different fathers is all," she shrugged as she pushed open the door. Then she turned back to him and her cheeks flushed pink.

"I'd rather have a cola if you've got one. Or water. Water would do."

She was suddenly much younger and less sure of herself. He smiled at her. "Not acquired a taste for real coffee yet?"

She shook her head.

He grabbed a couple of cans from the fridge and joined her on the step. Settling himself next to her, he handed her one of them. "Okay, cola it is. Now suppose you start by telling me your name…"

# Chapter Seven

Izzie was studying at the kitchen table when Jodie arrived home. Surrounded by papers and open textbooks, she barely acknowledged her. Jodie gave a tired smile as she bent down to unzip her riding boots. Kicking them into the corner she padded across to the sink in her socks and filled the kettle.

"Tea," she offered. "Or would you rather have juice?"

"Neither. I just had a drink," Izzie didn't lift her eyes from the page she was reading.

Although the table was remarkably clear of the usual clutter of mugs and biscuit crumbs that were part and parcel of her studies, Jodie didn't comment. Nor did she say anything about the bicycle propped against the porch, even though it was a giveaway. She had long ago learned to fight the battles that needed fighting and ignore the smaller skirmishes. It wasn't the end of the world if she had met up with a friend for a couple of hours just so long as she had spent most of the day revising for her exams.

Dropping a teabag into a mug of hot water, she sloshed it from side to side with a spoon. As she did so her mind went back to her own teenage years and she shuddered. Thank goodness Izzie was more level headed than she had been. She remembered the fights with her mother and her decision to leave home the moment she was old enough to follow her dream; a dream that had taken her so far away from her family that it had been almost twenty-four hours before she learned about the accident that had left her mother dead and her sister so mentally traumatized she was still afraid of the dark ten years later.

Flicking the teabag into the sink she walked across to the fridge for some milk. As she did so she noticed Izzie's shoulders were shaking.

Milk forgotten, she stopped by her sister's chair. "You're crying."

"Only because I'm happy."

Noticing the pile of scrunched up tissues on the table for the first time, Jodie frowned.

"Want to tell me about it?"

"Mmm…yes…I guess so," Izzie wriggled around in her chair. Then she pulled up her feet, wrapped her arms around her concertinaed legs and pressed her forehead into her knees.

Jodie's heart sank. This was Izzie's I know I'm in trouble pose. It was something she had done often when she was younger, a sort of 'head in the sand' action so she didn't have to look at Jodie. It was also something she hadn't done for a very long time. Jodie pulled out the chair opposite and lowered herself into it.

"I'm not going to like this am I?"

"Probably not," Izzie's reply was muffled. Then, while Jodie's mind was still flashing through a whole litany of negative scenarios, she lifted her head, squared her shoulders, and looked her in the eye.

"Marcus Lewis is going to give me music lessons," she said.

She might as well have said she was flying to the moon as far as Jodie was concerned.

"What do you mean, he's giving you music lessons? You haven't even met him."

"I have. I visited him this afternoon. I climbed the gate, just like you did," she added defiantly.

Noticing the smudges of mascara and the remnants of lipstick on her tearstained face, Jodie jerked forward and pulled down the neck of her sister's sweater. Beneath it she was wearing a sequined halter-top that showed more than it covered. It had been a bone of contention between them ever since she had found it in a charity shop and paired it with an equally miniscule skirt that showed off her long

35

legs to perfection and left little else to the imagination.

"What exactly have you been up to?" she demanded.

The eager expression on Izzie's face changed to a sullen frown. "I knew you'd be like this."

Jodie sat back with a sigh. "What did you expect? That I'd be delighted to learn you've visited a man old enough to be your father and spent time alone with him in his trailer? Whatever were you thinking of? He might have taken advantage of you. Celebrities like him are used to fans throwing themselves at them."

"He didn't though," Izzie's voice was small as she fingered the sweater. "He said I had to put this on and then he made me sit on the trailer steps with the door wide open. He said he wanted anyone passing by to be able to see me while we talked. He said he didn't want people thinking he let young girls visit his trailer on their own."

Then she grinned. "Only thing was, he forgot about the gate and the trespass sign. There weren't any passersby. There never will be any passersby."

Jodie stared at her. Then she smiled as relief washed over her. That it was about more than her sister's safety was something she didn't want to think about.

Izzie gave her a pleading look. "I can go can't I? Only he said he wouldn't give me lessons unless you said he could. He said to tell you to visit him and talk about it."

"Oh, he did, did he?" Jodie was surprised by the curl of warmth that coursed through her at the thought of meeting him again. "Well I suppose talking about it can't do any harm, so yes, I'll go and talk to him, even if it's just to apologize for the fact you turned up dressed to impress."

Like a ray of sunshine coming out, Izzie's face lit up. Her tear-washed eyes sparkled as she tumbled out of her chair and threw herself at Jodie in a tangle of arms and legs. Hugging her tightly she could feel the sharp bones of her ribs through the thick sweater. Her sister might be almost a head taller than her now. She might be difficult sometimes. But she was still the person she loved best in the world.

It was a thought that sometimes made her heart ache in

the middle of the night when she couldn't sleep. If it was this painful bringing up a sister, trying to get her safely through childhood and into adulthood, then she didn't think her battered heart would ever be able to cope with caring for children of her own.

# Chapter Eight

When he heard the gate rattle Marcus poked his head out of the trailer door.

"It's not locked," he called.

Startled by his voice, Jodie looked up, teetered on the top bar, and then tumbled down onto the driveway.

With a muttered exclamation he jumped down the steps and ran over to where she lay sprawled on the ground.

"Are you okay?" he asked, putting his hand out to pull her up.

Ignoring it, she stood up in one lithe movement and rescued her riding hat from where it had rolled across the path.

Marcus found himself openly staring at her hair. Until now it had always been tucked up out of sight, and despite wondering what color it was, he hadn't given it much thought. If anyone had asked him he would have guessed dark brown to match the bitter chocolate of her eyes, but he would never have imagined this. Black and glossy as a raven's wing, it hung in a thick plait that reached down to her waist, and he wanted to touch it.

Hurriedly averting his eyes, he forced himself to speak. "Are you sure you haven't hurt yourself?"

"I'm fine. If you ride horses, you get used to falling. I rolled. How was I meant to know the gate was unlocked though?"

He pointed as he unlatched it so she could lead her horse through. "No padlock, plus you could have left a message with the site manager to let me know you were coming."

She wrinkled her nose. "I was passing. Why the change of heart?"

"It's just a short term thing. I decided it wasn't doing a very good job keeping out unwanted visitors."

She looked slightly shamefaced. "I guess you mean Izzie and me."

He smiled down at her. "No harm done. I'm sorry I was so scratchy last time you were here. Come on in and have a coffee and let's see if we can start over."

"Maybe it would be better if I sat on the trailer steps," she said with the trace of a wicked smile.

He laughed. "I'll risk my reputation if you will."

She followed him into the trailer and sat on the couch. "Izzie isn't usually so stupid. She was trying to impress you when she turned up looking like her version of a celebrity. Oh I nearly forgot; your sweater is in Buckmaster's saddlebag. I'll go fetch it."

She started to get up again.

He caught her arm. "Give it to me later. There's no rush."

Then they both tried to pretend the physical contact meant nothing; that a spark of electricity hadn't just travelled down his arm and into hers. After a long moment he moved away and busied himself with mugs and coffee. When he turned back to her she didn't quite meet his eyes as she began to question him.

"What did Izzie say to you?"

"Mostly that she wants me to teach her stage craft. She says she has a fantastic voice."

She gave a wry smile. He could see she was deciding what to say to him. She sat forward once she had made up her mind.

"Did she tell you our mother died?"

He nodded.

"Did she tell you she was a singer too?"

"No, she didn't. She spent more time telling me why she needed to sing than filling me in on family stuff."

He could see the relief in her eyes when he told her that. It wasn't strictly true of course, but true enough. He had only gotten an outline from her sister, something about an accident and how Jodie had brought her up ever since.

39

"She did tell me you are her guardian though, and she said she would be in trouble once you knew she'd been here."

Jodie nodded, "She got that right. The thing is, Izzie's just like our mother. She was very beautiful and very talented too, but she was impulsive as well, and…and it destroyed her."

"And you are frightened the same thing will happen to your sister if she becomes a singer."

"Yes."

He waited.

"It's complicated. Izzie was in a car with her when it crashed. She saw her die. By then it was just the two of them because Izzie's father was dead and my mother's new boyfriend had abandoned them. I'd abandoned them too. I was working on the other side of the country and I was so caught up in my own life I hardly ever contacted them, so it was hours before anyone could track me down.

"By the time I reached the hospital Izzie was a complete basket case. She wouldn't speak or eat. She fought the nurses and doctors every time they touched her, so they had to sedate her most of the time. It was terrible. Fortunately, she doesn't remember much about it, but it doesn't mean it's gone away. She's nervy, and she's highly-strung. She doesn't sleep well. She can't sleep at all unless I'm close by. I'm already worried about how she'll cope when she goes away to university, so you see there's no way she'll ever be able to lead the life of a professional singer however much she thinks she wants to."

She stopped suddenly, as if she had run out of steam. He could see from the turmoil in her eyes she had given him an edited version of something she rarely spoke about.

"You must have been very young when all this happened," he said gently.

She gave a tired smile. "I was the same age Izzie is now. It's something she keeps bringing up every time I ask her to concentrate on her schoolwork and forget about her singing."

"That must have been tough. Was there no one else?"

40

"Nobody. But we got by. We're still getting by despite the teenage hormones because underneath it all she's a good kid."

He frowned. Although there was probably not much more than ten years between them, she seemed decades older than her sister. He wondered what she had given up to come home and take care of her. He wanted to ask but he sensed the subject was closed. She had told him what she thought he needed to know and now she wanted to talk about something else. He couldn't resist a final comment though. It was the same one he had made to Izzie.

"You don't look much alike."

"Different fathers is all," she shrugged as she repeated word for word what her sister had already told him. "Izzie's Dad, my stepfather, had Swedish ancestry from way back, so he was tall, with blue eyes and fair hair like Izzie. My father was short and dark apparently, not that I ever saw him."

"What happened?"

"He died before I was born."

He stirred his coffee thoughtfully. "Why didn't you tell the newspapers about Luke?"

She stared at him, thrown by the change of subject. "Why would I?"

"Because I won't open up the bridleway. It wasn't until after I told you about him that it occurred to me you might use it to get your own back."

"Not when you told me in confidence, I wouldn't. Anyway it's not Luke's battle is it, even though the newspapers would try to pretend it is? If they ever got hold of the story they would hang around all the time trying to get pictures of him and that wouldn't help anyone, least of all me."

He took a long drink of coffee as he struggled to come to terms with the sudden rush of gratitude that washed over him. He wasn't used to people being discreet or worrying about what was right or wrong. In his experience people usually just wanted to make money out of him.

"Thanks Jodie. I owe you."

"You really don't; but if you want to make Izzie happy, then listen to her sing. You only need to do it once."

"I will if it's what you want," he said. "But I don't want it to cause grief between the two of you."

"It won't do that. Refusing to let her do it is what would destroy us. So against my better judgment, I'm saying yes."

"Do you want to come too? As chaperone."

She laughed and shook her head as she stood up. "I'll just make sure she wears suitable clothes and you can leave the door open to protect your reputation. Remember what I've told you about her problems though and don't raise her hopes too high. I don't want her to abandon her plans for university. If you really want to do me a favor, then tell her a singing career is a really bad idea."

Instead of answering he scribbled something on a scrap of paper. "Here's my cell number. Tell her to call me. After I've listened to her I'll talk to you before I make any promises. That's if she's good enough of course."

"Oh she'll be good enough. She was right about that if nothing else." She twisted her plait up onto the top of her head and jammed her riding hat back on as she stood up.

He followed her to the door, grabbing an apple from a bowl of fruit on the way out. "I'll open the gate for you."

Buckmaster whickered as she walked up to him. She rubbed his nose. Then she reached into his saddlebag, pulled out the sweater, and handed it to Marcus.

He took it from her and then offered Buckmaster the apple. The chestnut gelding's response was so delicate that if he hadn't been watching he wouldn't have felt him take it from his outstretched palm.

"Hey, a new friend Bucky." She put her foot into the stirrup and swung herself onto the horse's back.

Marcus smiled up at her as he opened the gate. "See you then."

He watched her go and tried not to imagine what she might look like with her hair loose around her face. Then he clicked the gate shut and walked back to the trailer with his nose buried in the jumper.

# Chapter Nine

For the next two weeks Izzie was like a tightly drawn bow. She had contacted Marcus the moment Jodie gave her his cell number and then been devastated when he told her he was going to be away for ten days and she should phone him when he returned.

"I don't know how I'm going to wait," she wailed.

"You'll manage. You've enough homework to keep you busy. Marcus Lewis or no Marcus Lewis, you know I expect you to do well in your exams."

"Okay! Okay! You know I always work hard."

"Yes, I do." Jodie ruffled her hair. "I'm proud of you. Just don't get your hopes up too much about the music because Marcus Lewis is a busy man."

Izzie nodded. If that was what it was going to take to keep Jodie happy then she would nod until her head fell off. She would do anything for her except give up her plans because she knew that once he heard her sing she would be one step nearer to her dream.

* * *

Marcus knew it too. He knew it within the first few notes although he still put her through her paces. He made her sing a lot of different songs. He introduced jazz and soul. He played slow melodies. He played ragtime. It didn't matter. She was pitch perfect in all of them. And more confident than she had any right to be. The quality of her voice was mesmerizing too. Unexpectedly deep, it had a husky catch to it that was going to send a million teenagers crazy. She was raw and untrained of course, but that was almost incidental. Highly strung or not, he knew she had what it took to get right to the top.

When they had finished he left her to clear up the sheets of music scattered around his keyboard and walked over to the window. Outside he could see the shell of his music studio. Surrounded by scaffolding it was growing fast. He had made it his priority. That, and the ground floor suite he was having built for Luke. Everything else could wait. He was prepared to camp out in the trailer for as long as it took.

"I'm going to be away for a while," he told her, knowing she was waiting for him to say something. "I'll talk to Jodie when I get back."

When she didn't speak he turned around to look at her. Her face was pale and her fists were tightly clenched. Remembering what Jodie had said, he softened his tone.

"You don't need me to tell you how good you are Izzie. But you do need Jodie on side, and you also need to wait until my studio is finished. We can't achieve much inside this trailer with an electric keyboard. It's fine for composition but it doesn't do a lot for performance."

"But you are going to help me?" Her voice was little more than a hopeful whisper.

He nodded. "Oh yes, I'll help you if Jodie will let me, but you'll have to work hard. It's a tough life out there, with a lot of competition."

She nodded, her face tight with determination. "I'll do whatever it takes and nothing Jodie says will stop me."

* * *

Marcus sighed as he watched her wheel her bicycle towards the gate. What had he let himself in for? Just when he and Jodie had reached a truce of sorts he was going to have to unpick it all again by telling her it would be a crime to silence her sister's voice. Somehow he was going to have to persuade her to ignore her own fears and give Izzie a chance.

44

He looked at the numbers Izzie had scribbled on the pad on his desk. One was Jodie's phone number. His hand hovered over his cell. Should he call her now or should he wait until she had had a chance to talk to Izzie? An inexplicable need to hear her voice overruled common sense and he keyed in her number.

* * *

Jodie didn't recognize the number that flashed up on the screen when her phone rang. She knew it was Marcus Lewis as soon as he spoke though.

"I don't want you to say it," she told him, feeling her stomach plummet. "I don't want you to tell me how good she was. I don't want to think about it."

Hearing her echo his own thoughts, he gave a wry smile. "I won't then, but that's not why I called. I called to invite you to lunch."

Her silence was unnerving. Had he made a mistake? Was it just his imagination that had persuaded him the attraction was mutual?

"If it's not convenient now then we can make it later, when I come back."

"You're going away again?" His spirits rose when he heard the flatness in her voice.

"Yes, for six weeks. I have to go to America."

"What happens to Luke when you're away?"

Surprised by her question, he hesitated before he answered. "He stays at home in London with his care workers, just like he does when I come up here."

"How does he cope when you're not there?"

"Pretty well. I'm fairly incidental to his life. All he cares about is his daily routine."

He wondered if he was imagining disapproval in the silence that followed. Then she sighed. "Okay. I'll meet you for lunch but I've only got half an hour so it'll have to be a sandwich. I'll see you in the bar at the Station Inn at twelve-thirty."

He frowned as he pushed his cell phone back into his

pocket. Somehow she had managed to turn his lunch invitation around so that she seemed to be doing him a favor. It was almost as if she had only agreed to join him because she felt sorry for him. He gave a wry smile as he remembered all the girls who used to throw their underwear at him in the days when he still performed on stage, and the others who waited outside gigs for hours, even days, to get a glimpse of him arriving. And yet here he was, reduced to feeling grateful because a spiky woman who barely reached his shoulder was grudgingly prepared to spend half-an-hour with him; a woman who had caused him nothing but irritation and extra work ever since he met her; a woman who hadn't had a clue about him or his music until he closed her damned bridleway.

* * *

Marcus arrived at the inn twenty minutes early and sat at the bar nursing a glass of beer. It was quiet. No lunchtime crowd, which suited him. He glanced at the menu. All good rustic fare: a ploughman's platter with local cheeses; sandwiches with homemade bread; vegetable soup with fresh rolls. He wondered what Jodie would choose. Then he wondered if she often had lunch at the inn. Then he wondered why he couldn't stop thinking about her. He was still wondering when she pushed open the door and stepped inside.

Apart from dispensing with her riding hat she had made no concessions at all. No makeup, same clothes, same tidy plait down the centre of her back. It was quite obvious she didn't consider this a date. And if the frown on her face was anything to go by she didn't want to be here one little bit either. Feeling his good intentions begin to ebb away, Marcus waited for her to notice him. When she did, she approached him without a smile.

He slid off the bar stool and stood up. "We had better order straight away or you won't have time to eat. What would you like?"

"Just an orange juice please. And a cheese sandwich."

46

Last of the big spenders. Why didn't it surprise him? He placed their order and then nodded towards a nearby table. "Let's sit over there."

Looking as if she was about to be sick, she followed him, sat down in the chair opposite and immediately went on the attack. "Tell me what you've promised. Tell me what you said to Izzie. I need to know before I see her."

He shook his head, trying not to notice the soft swell of her breasts as she unzipped her shapeless fleece. Up until then he wouldn't have considered an emerald green T-shirt with some sort of official logo on the pocket to be one of fashion's great come-ons, but on Jodie it looked spectacular.

"Stop worrying. There's nothing to tell at the moment except what you already know, which is that your sister has a wonderful voice. I'm not about to spirit her away on a tour or anything. If she's serious about her singing then she has a lot to learn, and I can't even start thinking about it until the builders have completed my studio."

"You are going to help her then?"

"Maybe…but not before she's taken her exams. After that we'll take it one step at a time, and not without discussing it with you."

Seeing the tension drain out of her face he knew he had said the right thing. Now was not the time to tell her how exciting Izzie's voice was, how much it had thrilled the musician in him, and how, with the right advice and support, she had it in her to make it in the international music scene. One step at a time was what he was going to have to take with Jodie too.

For a fleeting moment he wondered how he had gotten himself so involved until another look at Jodie's face told him what he had been resisting until now. He wanted to get to know her better. She intrigued him as much as she attracted him. He wanted to find the real Jodie, the one who occasionally peeped out from behind her tough exterior in the trace of a dimpled smile or a flash of humor; and if he was going to be totally honest with himself, he also wanted to undo her glossy plait and run his fingers through her

47

hair.

The barmaid interrupted his thoughts by bringing plates of sandwiches to the table. After asking for a second beer, he started eating. Jodie took a bite from one of her sandwiches and then began to push crumbs of cheese around her plate.

"I don't mean to be so negative," she said. "My head knows she has to grow up and choose her own path but my heart doesn't seem to be listening. Every time I think of her out in the world on her own I get frightened. I keep remembering how she was after the accident and I know I couldn't bear for her to go through it again."

Surprised by the emotion in her voice, Marcus looked directly into her eyes, her green T-shirt, blue-black hair and tantalizing curves all forgotten. She met his gaze and he could see the fear there. He knew it wasn't a rational fear. Whatever it was, it was connected to the past, to the pieces she had left out of her story. He added *find out what really happened* to his Jodie 'to do' list. Right now though, all he wanted to do was take away the tormented expression in her pitch-dark eyes. He thrust his hand into the pocket of his jeans and brought out a key.

"This is for you. I almost forgot."

Jodie stared at it. Hope began to bloom deep inside her. "Is it what I think it is?"

"The key to the gate, yes. I decided if you could trust me with Izzie then I could trust you with my bridleway."

He held up his hand as she started to protest. "I know! I know! But technically it is my bridleway and I'm still not going to open it up to all and sundry. I'm prepared to let you use it while I'm away though, if it will help you to keep your young riders safe."

"And what about when you come back?"

He grinned at her. "You'll just have to wait and see won't you?"

She smiled at him then, a slow smile that started in her eyes and dimpled her cheeks before it reached the full curve of her lips. "Marcus…thank you."

She wasn't fulsome in her thanks, nor did she say

anything about how much easier it would make her life or how he was doing the right thing. She just said those three words, but they were enough because Marcus could see how much it meant to her and his heart lifted a little. It would have lifted further still if he didn't have to go away. It was bad enough having to leave Luke for long periods, but now, somehow, Jodie had wormed herself into the equation too. He wondered what she would say if he told her so.

# Chapter Ten

Carol stared at the key Jodie was holding. "Will that really unlock the gate to Marcus Lewis' bridleway?"

"It will. And as he's going to be away for ages, we won't even disturb him."

"You do realize what you've got there don't you? Keep it very safe Jodie because the newspapers, as well as his legion of fans, would kill for it. He knows they would jump at a chance to see where he's going to live, a chance to climb all over the scaffolding and take photos, so he must really trust you."

"I'd better keep it on a string around my neck then," Jodie gave a dismissive laugh as she curled her fingers protectively around the key.

Carol didn't return her smile. Instead she nodded approvingly. "That's a really good idea. I'm not joking. The fewer people who know you've got it, the better."

Jodie shook her head. "Don't worry. I've no intention of letting it out of my sight because I can't afford for anything to go wrong. As far as I'm concerned this is just the beginning. By the time I've finished Marcus will open up the bridleway to everyone."

"Good luck with that because I don't rate your chances once he's living there. I can't imagine he would find horses trailing past his house on a daily basis very inspirational."

* * *

Later, rummaging through a drawer in search of a ball of string, Jodie pondered Carol's words. She didn't really think she was right about the key. After all it was easy enough to climb over the gate, as she and Izzie had already proved, so what was the big deal? She would keep it on a string around her neck while she was working though, just to be on the safe side.

Finding the remnants of a ball of string at the very back of the drawer, she cut off a length, threaded it through the key, secured it with a knot, and then slipped the loop over her head. The key slithered its way past the buttons of her polo shirt to its chosen resting place between her breasts. She shivered as she recalled the moment Marcus had held it out to her in strong brown fingers. It had felt warm as she took it; warm from his hand, warm from the pocket of his jeans, warm from Marcus.

She busied herself by tidying up the various items the instructors had left strewn across the table in their hurry to get to lessons. Then she dried up the mugs draining beside the sink and returned them to the cupboard next to the coffee, tea and sugar canisters. She wasn't going to think; not about Izzie and her singing; not about the key; and definitely not about Marcus.

\* \* \*

Two hours later, still not thinking about Marcus, she tried to unlock the gate to the bridleway while a straggle of horses, riders and instructors waited patiently in the lane behind her.

Marcus paused in the middle of loading his final piece of luggage into the boot of his car and watched her struggle with the key. It was a large key and the lock was stiff. When she failed at the third attempt he abandoned his bag and strode up the driveway towards her.

"Here, let me. I should have remembered it was difficult to turn. I'll get the site manager to oil the lock for you."

She handed it to him without a word. Their fingers brushed as he took it from her and a shot of unexpected desire jolted him. Beside him he heard Jodie's tiny intake of breath.

As the key clicked into place he looked at her. There was a flush of color in her smooth olive skin and her eyes, so dark they were almost black, were full of...what? Was it desire or was it fear, or was it something far more complicated? He couldn't be sure because as soon as the gate swung open she turned away and began to chivy her ragtag battalion onto the bridleway.

He sighed as he locked the gate behind them. Then he called out to her. "Haven't you forgotten something?"

Jodie handed the reins of the horse she was leading to one of the instructors and ran back to where he was standing, the key swinging from his fingers.

"Sorry," she said, taking it from him. He watched as she slipped the loop of string over her head and tucked the key inside her polo shirt. Trying not to think about where it was resting, he took hold of her hand. His grip tightened as she tried to pull away.

"Jodie, hear me out. I hope I'm not speaking out of turn but I want to spend more than a quick half-hour with you when I get back. Can we do that?"

She stared up at him and he could feel her resistance, see the refusal beginning to shape her lips. He shook his head. "Don't say it! Don't say anything. Just think about it while I'm away will you? And when I come back I'll ask you again."

They stared at one another for a long moment, and then she nodded. He kept her hand clasped in his as he walked her back to her horse. Both of them ignored the wide-eyed curiosity of the riders and the envious sighs of two of the instructors: Marcus because he didn't care, and Jodie because she didn't notice.

* * *

To all outward appearances life very quickly went back to normal once Marcus left. When Izzie wasn't studying she spent most of her spare time helping out at the stables, either mucking out the horses or leading some of

52

the younger children around the training ring. It was something she enjoyed doing, and Jodie encouraged it because the children loved working with her.

Jodie herself, busy with end of year accounts as well as all the everyday tasks that managing the riding school entailed, barely managed to fit in mealtimes let alone any leisure activity. It was the same every year when the onset of warmer weather and sunshine tempted new riders out of winter hibernation.

Neither of them mentioned Marcus; Izzie because she didn't want to have a discussion about her future with Jodie; Jodie because she didn't want to think about him at all. She managed fairly well during the day but at night, lying alone in her bed staring up at the ceiling, it was altogether more difficult. With no other distractions she found she couldn't ignore the memory of the pressure of his fingers on hers, the way his eyes crinkled at the corners when he smiled, the shadow of a cleft in his chin. And often, when she woke up in the morning, she blushed to discover he'd been the shadowy figure in her dreams.

\* \* \*

It wasn't until a journalist from the local paper called to ask how her campaign was progressing that Jodie had to confront how she really felt about Marcus, however. Still militant as far as the bridleway was concerned, she ignored Carol's warning and told him about the key, and about how she hoped the temporary arrangement would soon become permanent, reconciling her twinge of guilt about mentioning it at all with a need to keep the issue in the public eye. It was a discussion she soon regretted though, because when she approached the gate an hour or so later, he was waiting for her.

"I'm here to give your campaign a boost," he said as he pointed a camera at the straggle of horses and riders following her.

Irritated, Jodie jumped down from her horse and stood in front of the viewfinder. "You can't do that, not without

53

permission. They're just children."

"All right, keep your hat on. I'll take a back view of them as they ride down the path."

Knowing there was nothing she could do to stop him, Jodie shrugged and unlocked the gate. She had started the campaign after all, so it didn't make any kind of sense to refuse some publicity. Besides, Marcus might change his mind again, so she needed to keep the local paper on side.

The photographer stood back as the children rode past. Then, true to his word, he took several shots of them disappearing down the bridleway. Anxious to lock the gate behind her so she could rejoin the children and the other instructors, Jodie fidgeted impatiently as he adjusted his lens.

"Surely you've taken enough," she said, starting to lead Buckmaster through the gate.

"Of the children, yes. Not of Marcus Lewis' house though. How fantastic to get to see what's going on behind the gates while he's not here. Trespassing wouldn't be good for the paper, but with you here it's legitimate. You're a star Jodie. How did you persuade him to give you the key? No! On second thoughts I don't think I want to know."

It took Jodie several moments to register the sexual implication behind his words. When she did, she flushed scarlet. He chuckled as he tried to push past her. "Don't worry, your secret's safe with me."

"How dare you!" She used Buckmaster to block the gateway, determined to protect Marcus' privacy. She could cope with a slur on her reputation if that was how the journalist was going to play it, but she had no intention of letting Marcus down. Besides, he would be furious if photos and a description of the building work appeared in the local paper just because he'd trusted her with the key. It was one thing to talk about the bridleway, quite another to allow the journalist through the gate. Apart from anything else it would put an end to any hope she had that he'd eventually reconsider. If she let him down she could wave goodbye to the path ever being reopened permanently.

"Wait until Mr. Lewis comes home and ask him to

show you around himself," she pleaded, hoping an appeal to the man's better judgment would achieve more than losing her temper, despite the provocation.

"You must be joking. Everyone knows he's very tight lipped as far as his private life is concerned, so this is probably my only chance. Just look the other way Jodie."

"No! You can't do this. It's still trespassing because I promised I wouldn't let anybody else onto the bridleway."

He ignored her as he tried to push past Buckmaster. When the horse resisted, he slapped it on the flank. Buckmaster's snort of fury prompted Jodie to hang on tightly to the reins.

"What do you think you're doing?"

"I already told you. I'm going to take some photos of the house. And if you want the paper to carry on supporting your campaign then you'd better keep your damned horse under control."

"My horse is fine. It's you who is out of order."

The skirmish rapidly degenerated into a slanging match with Buckmaster moving restlessly between them. Jodie was at her wits end. She couldn't close the gate without loosening her grip on the reins, and anyway the journalist was already standing foursquare on the bridleway and showing every sign of being prepared to wait her out. Torn between a need to pacify Buckmaster and a wish to punch her opponent right in the middle of his self-satisfied face, she was relieved to hear footsteps approaching from behind.

"Are you having problems Miss?" The voice belonged to Bill, Marcus' site manager, a very large man whose face wore a permanent frown. He waved to Jodie whenever she rode by but, until now, had never offered anything more than a grunt of verbal acknowledgement.

Still intent on Buckmaster who was steadily becoming more and more agitated, Jodie gave him a grateful glance. "I've been trying to tell this man he can't take photographs of the house, not without permission."

"He can't even come onto the property without permission." Bill's voice matched his bulk. Deep and sonorous, and accompanied by a fierce scowl, its effect was instantaneous. Within moments the photographer had retreated to the lane and Bill had clicked the gate shut behind him. When Jodie tried to thank him, he just winked and walked away. He told Marcus though.

* * *

The call came while she was getting ready for bed.

"Jodie. It's Marcus." The leap of her heart even before he said his name shocked her into momentary silence.

"Bill called me. He said you had a bit of trouble with the Press today. Jodie…are you there?"

"I'm…yes…I'm here. He shouldn't have bothered you. It was fine."

"It didn't sound like that to me. Bill said the journalist was trying to bully you."

"He was until he saw Bill and decided he needed to be somewhere else in a hurry!"

She heard the laughter in his voice when he answered her. "Size wins I guess. He said you were doing a pretty good job on your own until he arrived though."

"Well I've had a lot of practice. Battles are my thing in case you haven't noticed."

She spoke lightly but Marcus sensed an underlying tension. His voice softened. "I have noticed, and I understand about the bridleway, I really do… but it's not just that is it?"

There was a long silence before she sighed. "No, it's not just that, but it's complicated."

"Try me."

When it became obvious she wasn't going to answer he searched for some neutral words to keep her on the other end of the phone. "How's Buckmaster?"

Her peal of laughter was reward enough. "He's fine even though you don't really want to know."

"I do," he protested. Then, before commonsense kicked in and stopped him, he added the words that had been haunting him ever since he last saw her. "I want to

56

know everything about you Jodie. I want to know about your life. I want to know what you think. I want to spend time with you without that infernal riding hat."

The silence was back. He sighed. What else had he expected? She didn't know him, not really. He was just a guy who was hitting on her and he was a fool to think she was ready for that from someone who had not only shut off her beloved bridleway without a thought for the people who used it, but who was about to disrupt her life even more by encouraging her sister to sing.

"I'm sorry Jodie. I had no right…it came out all wrong. I already told you I want to get to know you better though, so I'm not going to pretend I don't, but long distance from America is probably not the best way to follow through. Tell me about Buckmaster instead. Where did you get him because even I can see he's a fine horse?"

"I…he was a present. Someone I used to work for gave him to me when I left the job I was doing to take care of Izzie."

"That's some leaving present! They must have valued you a great deal."

"Not really. Bucky was lame. He'd had an accident. The owner was talking about having him put down." Her voice trailed off.

Marcus could see it all. The handsome chestnut favoring one leg, the owner no longer prepared to spend good money on a poor prospect, and Jodie, small and fierce, standing protectively in front of Buckmaster arguing for his life. He smiled.

"Another battle huh?"

"Mmm." She wasn't about to have a long intimate conversation with him but he could sense she wasn't about to cut the call either.

"So how long did it take to get him fit?"

"About a year. I negotiated a 'feed Bucky for free' clause when I signed my contract with the riding school!"

He laughed out loud. "Why doesn't that surprise me? I can already see my chances of winning the battle of the bridleway fading into the distance."

"Do you really mean that?" From the sudden animation in her voice he knew she was smiling. He remembered how that looked. Her eyes would be shining and there would be a dimple at the corner of her mouth. He wanted to keep that expression on her face and suddenly he knew he wanted it a lot more than he wanted his privacy.

"I'll find a way to keep it open and protect Luke from nosy journalists," he promised. "Now tell me more about Buckmaster. What happened once his leg healed? Did you start using him for lessons?"

"No. He's much too temperamental. I wouldn't trust him with just anyone. Bucky's a one-person horse except for when he's around disabled children. Then it's as if he remembers what it was like to be lame and has decided it's payback time. He's so patient and gentle that all the children love him."

Remembering how the big, handsome chestnut whickered a soft greeting whenever it saw Jodie approaching, and remembering, too, how delicately it had taken the apple from his hand, Marcus smiled. Buckmaster and Jodie were two of a kind. Both feisty, both battle scarred, and both complete suckers when it came to the underdog. They were both in need of gentling too. His heart bucked as his imagination kicked into overdrive and conjured up pictures of Jodie lying trustingly in his arms while he covered her eyelids with the softest of kisses before…with an effort he pulled himself together and searched for another question.

"How does that work? He's a big horse."

"It just does. He will stand still for hours while they make a fuss of him. He gets more apples and carrots than any other horse at the stables. All the children come with their pockets stuffed to bursting."

"So what about this riding program? Explain it to me."

There was a pause and then she laughed. "You don't get away with it that easily Marcus Lewis. Come and find out for yourself when you get back."

\* \* \*

58

Marcus was thoughtful when they cut the call twenty minutes later. Maybe he would check out the disabled riding program. Not for Luke because that was never going to happen, but so he could see Jodie at work. It would give him a chance to get to know her better which was something he definitely wanted to do.

He stared out of the window, his cell phone halfway to his pocket. Who had given her that horse? She had said his name when she talked about a stable she had once worked in. Stephen something? Stephen…Robson…Roberts? That was it, Stephen Roberts. Where had he heard that name before?

"The studio is waiting for you Mr. Lewis," the girl who had been assigned to look after him for the whole of his stay pushed open the door and gave him an anxious smile.

"Sorry, I was on a call," he apologized as he joined her in the doorway. "I'll get over there right away."

Then he paused. "Would you do me a favor? Would you go onto the Internet and see what you can find out about a Stephen Roberts? He's something to do with horses…probably a horse trainer in the UK or maybe he runs a riding school. And while you're at it, do a search on a Jodie Eriksson too. There will be some sort of connection between them."

# Chapter Eleven

"What happened to stop you competing?" Marcus didn't waste time with small talk when he called Jodie the following day. He was too angry about whatever it was that had ended her career as a junior dressage rider just at the point she was about to make it into the big time.

When he'd returned to his hotel at the end of the studio session, a sheaf of papers was waiting for him; printouts about Stephen Roberts and Jodie. As he'd half suspected, Stephen Roberts was the owner of a highly successful livery stable. Jodie must have trained there in the days when she was the future of British dressage. Amongst the papers he'd found articles detailing her successes with the British junior team and a lot of commentary about her prospects. There were also interviews with Jodie herself, and pictures of her as a teenager. In some she was holding a trophy high above her head, in others she had a medal around her neck, and in every single one of them she had an expression of absolute joy on her face. Marcus had stared at them for a long time. Now he wanted to know where that joy had gone and why she was no longer competing. Given the dates of the articles he was sure it wasn't just because she'd had to start taking care of Izzie.

"The money ran out," Jodie's voice was flat. She didn't seem to be surprised by his question. "When my step-father died he left a pile of debts and a failing business behind him, so the horses had to go along with everything else."

"I'm so sorry Jodie. I read all about you, about how you won the Pony European Dressage Championships

60

when you were only fourteen. I read about the hopes you had for the future too, but then you disappeared. No more news about you at all."

"That's because I became old news as soon as I stopped competing."

"I don't know what to say," Marcus almost wished he hadn't started the conversation because he had obviously stirred up painful memories.

"You don't need to say anything. It was all a very long time ago. A lot has happened since then…too much for something like a career in dressage to matter very much."

He didn't believe her. Nobody could be that good and just walk away without regrets.

"It must have been difficult."

"I don't want to talk about it," he could hear the finality in her voice.

"Let's talk about now then. How long have you been running the riding school?"

"About six years. Before that I was an instructor, although I don't know why I'm telling you this."

"You're telling me because you know how I feel about you Jodie."

She was silent for so long he began to think she'd cut the call. Then he heard her sigh. "I don't want to talk about that either Marcus," she said.

He gave a wry smile, wondering if he had gone a step too far, too soon. "What shall we talk about then?"

"Let's talk about you. What are you doing in America? How is Luke coping without you?"

"Luke is fine. I already told you he just needs routine, and I pay people to supply that. I'm nothing more than an incidental in his life."

"I don't believe you."

"Sadly it's true, but I've learned to live with it."

'I don't believe that either."

"Are you always this good at stopping conversations mid-flow?"

"It depends on the conversation. Maybe if you told me about your work I would be so spellbound I would forget to interrupt." She surprised him with a sudden bubble of laughter in her voice.

"Challenge accepted," he said. "I'm in the middle of composing a film score for Patrice O'Brien. The film is about a boy who travels across America in search of his father. I have to come up with music that has quite a bit of pathos as well as a lot of feel-good factor, and I have less than six weeks to do it. I'm working eighteen hour days out here Jodie."

The silence was back but this time he knew she was teasing him. He chuckled.

"Okay. You've proved your point. You're spellbound! What else do you want to know?"

"How you do it? Do you work with the actors on set, or with the film?"

"It varies. This time around I'm working with the film. I spent most of today watching the rushes and then discussing the story with Patrice."

* * *

By the time they ended the call Marcus had given Jodie a Master Class on how to compose a film score. He smiled as he pushed his cell phone back into his pocket. He could think of a number of people who would kill to hear what he had just told her about his work, whereas Jodie hadn't been impressed at all. Interested yes, but not impressed. She hadn't even cared that Patrice O'Brien was one of the most famous film directors around. It was just another job to her, the sort of job a musician did. Marcus Lewis the international star was an irrelevance.

What was it she had said…that she'd become old news as soon as she stopped competing? Well he was old news too, as far as performance was concerned. His film scores were the only things that kept him in the public eye nowadays. Jodie had never even heard of him before he disrupted her life and he was surprised to discover how much it pleased him. After so long in the public eye it was a relief to be treated as a regular guy who was just doing

62

his job. He also liked the fact she hadn't protested when he said he would call her again the following day.

* * *

For the next two weeks he called her every evening at the same time, just as she was climbing into bed. Although he didn't have much choice due to the time difference as well as their busy work schedules, he still liked the thought of it. Every time she answered the phone he wanted to ask her what she was wearing and whether her hair was loose. He wanted to ask her if she was sitting in a chair or lying on her bed. He wanted to know if she had waited anxiously for his call or whether she had forgotten about it until the phone rang. For his own self-preservation, however, he didn't ask her any of those things. Instead he talked about his day and asked her about hers, and slowly, with Jodie testing him every step of the way, they became friends.

That he spent the whole time he was talking to her imagining her with her hair spread across her pillows and her body warm and rosy from a shower was the one thing he didn't share with her. Instead he told her about the view from his hotel window. He described Hollywood. He made her laugh with stories about some of the celebrities he had seen cruising the boulevards. And he missed her the minute he cut the call.

* * *

"I guess that's lover boy again," Izzie stuck her head around Jodie's bedroom door with a grin.

Jodie scowled at her. "Go to bed."

"As if," she climbed onto the bed, hugged her knees to her chest and waited with an expectant grin on her face.

"I'm not answering it," Jodie told her. "Not unless you go away."

"Not a problem," Izzie leaned forward, plucked the phone from her hand and pressed the call button.

"Hi Marcus. How's life in Hollywood?"

"It's good. What about your exams?"

Izzie sighed. "And here I was thinking you might mistake me for Jodie and whisper some sweet nothings into my ear!"

Outraged, Jodie attempted to snatch the phone. Izzie laughed as she held it out of reach.

"Gotta say goodbye now Marcus. Jodie's not happy. I'll leave you to calm her down." She tossed the phone onto the bed as she untangled her legs and made for the door. She was still chuckling as she slammed it shut behind her.

"Your sister needs to learn some respect," Marcus told Jodie when she picked up the phone. He was laughing. Jodie wasn't. Her face was scarlet with mortification and her lips were quivering.

How could Izzie have done that to her? How did she even know Marcus kept calling? Had she been listening at the bedroom door?

"I'm sorry," she whispered. "She had no right."

"Hey, don't let it upset you. She's just a kid."

"She's still old enough to know better." Although the color had faded from her cheeks, Jodie's voice was shaking.

"Maybe she does…know better I mean. Maybe she's just trying to push you in the direction I'm trying to lead you. I want to whisper sweet nothings into your ear. You know I do. I want you Jodie."

"Don't Marcus. And please don't call me any more…I…I can't do this."

\* \* \*

It was three days before Marcus managed to speak to her again. Three days of ignored calls. Three days where she deleted every single voice mail without listening to it.

Izzie cracked first. She had spent every moment since that fatal phone call making silent atonement. Her bedroom was so tidy she could actually find things. She hadn't demurred when Jodie suggested extra studying either. Nor had she complained when one of the stable girls

64

went down with a stomach bug and she had to get up an hour earlier to help out with the horses before school. She'd done all the washing up too, without being asked, but enough was enough. If Jodie wouldn't talk to her about it, then maybe Marcus would.

Removing her sister's cell phone from the breakfast table when her back was turned, she found Marcus' number and called him. He answered straight away.

"Jodie?"

"No. It's Izzie. Marcus I'm sorry. I didn't mean to upset you."

"You didn't upset me. It's Jodie you need to apologize to."

"I've tried, but she won't talk about it. Actually she's not really talking about anything much right now. That's why I'm calling. I don't know what else to do."

"Where is she?"

"Outside with Bucky. She's saddling him up for his morning ride. She doesn't know I've taken her phone."

Thanking the god of small mercies that Izzie seemed to be devoid of any sort of moral compass when it came to other people's property, Marcus allowed himself a moment of hope.

"Perhaps you'd better return it."

"You'll talk to her?"

"Of course I will, if she'll let me. Just take the phone out to her."

"Okay," he could hear the relief in her voice. Then the tension came back. "Why is she doing this Marcus? Why won't she speak to you?"

"Because she's scared."

"Scared because I want to sing? Scared because I'm going to leave home?"

His voice was sharp as he replied. "Although you might find this difficult to accept, not everything revolves around you, even though your sister makes it seem that way. This is about Jodie and her feelings."

"Her feelings for you?"

He sighed. "Maybe. Now take me out to her please,

65

before she sets off."

He heard a lot of background noises as she zipped up her school bag, grabbed her blazer, and hurried out into the yard. Then he heard the sharp clop of a horse's hooves on the paving and a muffled conversation. Suddenly Izzie's voice was clear again.

"Gotta run. The school bus will be here any minute. Bye Jodie." There was a pause, and then she added, "Oh, I nearly forgot. Here's your phone. You left it on the table. You've got a call."

He grinned. Trespasser, thief, liar, was there no end to her criminal tendencies? Then he forgot all about her because Jodie was on the phone.

"Jodie its Marcus. Please don't hang up...and don't be cross with Izzie either because she's only doing what she thinks is right. She's worried about you and so am I."

"Well you don't need to be. I'm fine. I just think it's better if we take a break. I'll have to talk to you when you get back won't I, because of Izzie's music, and because you're coming to the stables to check out the riding program."

Despite himself, he chuckled. "You're nothing if not tenacious. I thought you'd have forgotten about that by now."

"Not a chance, not when I'm sure it will do Luke some good."

"Okay. You win, but on two conditions. The first is that you stop blocking my calls, and the second is you meet Luke before you start making any plans for him."

"Done. And I'm sorry I stopped talking to you. I don't mean to be so prickly. I guess Izzie just caught me at a raw moment."

"No she didn't. She scared you." Having got this far he wasn't going to let her shy away from the truth. "She made you face up to your feelings Jodie and they frighten you."

"You're an expert are you, on other people's feelings?" her reply was tart.

"Yes. I've had so much therapy I am about as much of

an expert as you are ever likely to meet. I know about scared too, because for years I was scared every single day. It's why I gave up performing."

* * *

Three weeks later Jodie urged Buckmaster into a gallop and then gave him his head. He raced down the deserted beach, his mane and tail flying in the wind as he kicked up little puffs of sand behind him. Laughing out loud, she reveled in the clear blue sky and the crash of the waves on the shore.

"Marcus is coming home today, Bucky," she told him. "And guess what? I'm not scared anymore…well maybe I am a little bit…but in a good way."

Buckmaster snorted, as he always did when Jodie spoke to him. She tweaked his ears affectionately. "You see he's got hang-ups too, and responsibilities, so he understands how I feel."

"His wife died when Luke was two, and Marcus blames himself. He says he went away a lot and left her to cope with Luke on her own. He says he didn't even notice when she became depressed because he was too busy touring. He had no idea she was taking anti-depressants as well as other drugs until she took an overdose. He doesn't think she meant to, not really, but he'll never know for sure, and that's why he can't forgive himself."

Buckmaster slowed to a walk. He was breathing heavily. Jodie leaned forward and pressed her face against his neck. "And it's why he can't perform anymore either. He's scared that if he does, something bad will happen to Luke. It doesn't make any sort of sense but I guess that's what hang-ups are all about Bucky. They don't make sense…they just are."

They reached the bottom of the bridleway as she finished speaking and she slowed to a gentle pace so she could see the latest progress on Marcus' house. The studio was taking shape now and the builders were busy digging the foundations for another structure a few meters away.

Marcus had explained about the glass corridor linking the two buildings. He had explained about the swimming pool too, and the gym, as well as the specially equipped ground floor suite for Luke.

"Swimming is good for him," he said when she teased him about his grandiose plans. "And he needs the gym for his physiotherapy. He suffers from poor coordination and balance plus a whole host of other minor difficulties so regular exercise is an essential part of his routine."

She had stopped teasing him once she realized he didn't like it...not when it was about Luke. Instead she asked him about the rest of the design and been impressed with the comparative modesty of his own needs. The studio and Luke's pool and gym complex would dwarf the rest of the house.

A huge covered truck was blocking the road as she approached the end of the bridleway. Bill was talking to the driver but when he saw her he stepped forward and unlocked the gate. Smiling her thanks, she guided Buckmaster through.

He nodded towards the truck. "Those are for you."

The rear doors were open and Jodie stared inside in disbelief. The interior of the truck was crammed with row after row of laurel bushes, each one at least eight feet tall.

"They're for the bridleway, to stop people looking in," he explained, waving in the general direction of the driveway to where trench had been dug along the full length of the wire fence separating it from the path.

She grinned at him. "He doesn't do things by halves does he? Those bushes must have cost a fortune."

# Chapter Twelve

The rest of the day dragged. Apart from one short text telling her his plane had landed safely, Marcus hadn't contacted her. Knowing he had meetings with his agent and with his recording studio, and accepting he had to spend time with Luke, Jodie tried hard not to mind. Besides, commonsense told her he would have far less free time now he was back into his everyday life. There would be no more late night phone calls, no more confidences shared. He would be too busy.

After twenty-four hours she started panicking. "I can't remember what he looks like," she whispered to Buckmaster as she tightened his girth. "I can't even remember what he sounds like anymore."

Buckmaster blew into her ear and then nuzzled her pocket, hoping to find a carrot. She pushed him away with a sigh. What a fool she had been. Why on earth had she spent so much time talking to Marcus when anyone with an ounce of sense would have realized he was just filling in time until he could return home and get on with his life?

"Come on Bucky," she led the chestnut horse out of his stable. "Let's go and see if those laurel bushes have been planted yet. At least he's kept his promise about finding another way to protect Luke from people using the bridleway."

* * *

The gate was open when she and Buckmaster arrived and the lane outside was full of men wearing safety boots and fluorescent jackets. Some were unloading another truck of laurel bushes and others were re-routing the footpath that led to the bridleway.

Anxious to get her horse past all the activity before he was spooked, Jodie dug her heels into his flanks and directed him through the open gateway. As she did so she wondered how much all this extra work was going to cost. Not that it would faze Marcus, not when he was already spending a fortune on his house and studio. For the first time she considered what it meant and her thoughts grew even darker.

Marcus Lewis was famous and he was rich. He probably had more money than anyone she knew. More money even than the wealthy trainers she had worked for in the past. Far more money than her stepfather in the days when he had bought her whatever she wanted, whenever she wanted; so why on earth was he bothering with her? Was it to keep her sweet so she wouldn't tell the Press about Luke? That must be it because she had absolutely nothing else to offer him. She was nobody. She couldn't compete with his world of glamour and celebrity, nor did she want to. She wanted to stay in the village, living with Izzie, and running the riding school. They might not have much money but at least they were safe. Izzie was safe.

Thinking of her sister reminded Jodie of Marcus again and she scowled. She might have given in over the music lessons but only because Izzie wanted them so badly, not because she wanted to please him. There was no way she was going to sign up to any plans he might have to encourage Izzie onto the stage.

Buckmaster, sensing her tension, quickened his pace. Automatically she reached down to pat him. As she did so she found herself looking into a pair of bright blue eyes. Marcus was leaning against a tree. He looked just the way he had before panic had erased his features from her memory. He was tall, tan, and far too attractive, and she wanted to get past him as quickly as possible.

"You're late today. I was worried I'd missed you or you'd taken another route."

She shook her head and wished her tongue hadn't suddenly stuck itself to the roof of her mouth. She had forgotten how the silver frosting on his hair contrasted with the blue of his eyes. Forgotten how his lean, angular frame and sharp cheekbones gave him a look of moody mystery. Forgotten how much his face lit up when he smiled. He was smiling now but his smile slowly faded when she didn't respond.

"Jodie? Is something the matter?"

She shook her head again. It wasn't important she had lost the power of speech because how could she tell him she had already given up on him. How could she say she didn't believe all the things he had told her, all those words about how much he wanted her, about how he was counting the days until he could see her again? All of it had been fantasy, the fantasy of someone alone and lonely, and three thousand miles away. If those long distance conversations had taken place in the clear light of day instead of in the dark intimacy of her bedroom she would never have fallen for a single word. With something close to a sob, she kicked Buckmaster's flanks. She needed to get away.

Marcus was too quick for her. Producing an apple from his pocket he held it out. Buckmaster, torn between obedience to Jodie and his own greed couldn't resist it. As he took the apple with a whicker of pleasure, Marcus grabbed hold of his rein.

"I'm not letting go until you get off and talk to me," he told Jodie. "I don't care if you drag me all the way down to the beach with you."

At her third shake of the head Marcus put his hand on her riding boot. His voice hissed with anger and frustration.

"Get down and tell me what's the matter Jodie. I thought we'd gotten over all this. I thought you wanted to see me as much as I wanted to see you."

"I do. I did," she croaked, swallowing hard against the dryness in her throat.

"So what's changed?"

"Me. I've changed Marcus. I've had time to see how it really is between us. How all that midnight talk was

71

because you were lonely and I was flattered. I…you don't want me, not really. I wouldn't fit into your life. I'd…"

His eyes blazing, Marcus tugged at the stirrup. "Is this what happens when I don't call you for one day? If it is then what you've just said is true. You won't fit into my life, not if you don't trust me. Not if you don't believe I meant every word I said to you.

"I've knocked myself out to get here this soon Jodie. I went straight from the airport to the meetings in London I told you about. Then I spent time with Luke. Not nearly enough time, but sufficient to remind him who I am. After that I grabbed a couple of hours sleep, just enough to make sure I could stay awake on the motorway; just enough so I could drive safely through the night and be here in time to surprise you on your early morning ride. But if that's not enough for you then I guess you're right. We're done."

He let go of her foot and the bridle as he finished speaking, and turned away.

Jodie stared down at him. "You did all that…for me?"

This time it was his turn to give a silent nod.

"Marcus…I'm sorry."

He turned back to look at her. This time his eyes were a dull grey, and he looked older. He looked, she thought, as if someone had punched him. His shoulders drooped and there were dark smudges of exhaustion under his eyes.

Without another thought she kicked her feet out of the stirrups and slithered off Buckmaster's broad back. Relieved of his load, and aware that Jodie was no longer concentrating on him, he wandered over to a patch of grass and began munching.

Standing in front of Marcus she took a deep breath. "I wish I didn't have to keep saying I'm sorry but I'm not very good at trust because…because of things that happened in the past. If you'll give me another chance maybe I can learn not to be so touchy."

"You mean that?" He kept his hands firmly in his pockets.

She gave him a tentative smile. "Yes I do."

They stared at one another for the briefest moment and

72

then she was in his arms and he was kissing her. It was a kiss that went on for a very long time. It dislodged her riding hat until Marcus unclipped it and tossed it to the ground. It drew small whimpering moans from Jodie as he slipped his hands inside her shapeless green fleece. It made Marcus forget everything except the softness of her skin, the taste of her lips and the dance of her tongue against his. It was a kiss that had been waiting for a long time, a kiss that had started three thousand miles away. Now it had reached its destination, Marcus and Jodie were oblivious to their surroundings.

* * *

Buckmaster was bored. He had finished the patch of grass, sampled a laurel leaf and decided he didn't like it, and rubbed his rump against the fence post to deal with an irritating itch. Now he wanted Jodie. He trotted back up the path to where she was standing with the apple man and nudged her with his nose. When it had no effect he gave a snort of indignation and blew into her ear.

"I could almost believe that horse is jealous," Marcus kept Jodie in the circle of his arms as she turned towards Buckmaster. Happy that his beloved mistress was concentrating on him again, the horse lifted his top lip in what was a very good impersonation of a leer.

When they had stopped laughing Marcus tilted Jodie's chin and dropped a kiss onto the tip of her nose. "I guess he's right. This is not the time or the place. Bill will come looking for me soon to bring me up to speed about the building work. I told him I was going for a walk."

Jodie sighed. "I'm busy all day today too, and I've still got to take Bucky down to the beach."

"What about this evening."

She shook her head. "I have to go to Izzie's school to see her teacher."

"Problems?"

"No, it's just an end of term meeting. A general discussion about how well she's expected to do in her exams, what university she might want to apply to, that sort of thing."

He pulled her to him and rested his chin on the top of her head so she couldn't see his face. Now wasn't the time to tell her that he'd known Izzie wouldn't be going to university from the moment he first heard her sing. "I guess it has to be another late night phone call then."

She tilted her face up and gave him a rueful smile. For the first time he noticed that her eyelashes curled. He noticed, too, that she had a tiny mole just above her left eyebrow. He bent and kissed it.

"There is another way of course. Come back to London with me tomorrow and stay for the weekend…it'll mean you can meet Luke too."

She shook her head. "I can't leave Izzie on her own, not over a weekend…not ever really."

He didn't comment other than to say that of course her sister was invited too, because he didn't want to have any sort of conversation about Izzie's future. Besides, if she came as well then he'd be able to listen to her in a fully equipped studio.

# Chapter Thirteen

"Please pinch me!" Izzie thrust her arm under Jodie's nose and screwed her eyes tight shut. "Unless you pinch me hard I won't believe it!"

"What? That we're going to stay with Marcus." Jodie laughed at her.

"How can you be so casual? We are not going to stay with Marcus. We are going to London to stay with Marcus Lewis. Just wait 'til I tell all my friends. They'll be green with envy."

"You won't have an opportunity to tell them anything at all unless you hurry up and get ready. We need to leave in three minutes or we'll be late for our appointment."

"It's such a waste of time," Izzie grumbled as she shrugged her arms into a thick sweater and finger combed her hair in front of the mirror. "You know exactly what she's going to say because she says it every time. Isabella is such an asset to the school and such a credit to you Ms Eriksson. I'm sure she'll do well in her exams and be accepted by whatever university she chooses."

Although Jodie chuckled at Izzie's accurate impersonation of the school principal, she still shook her head. "Let's hope she's right then, because you need to do well. University is going to be a tough call. You'll have to learn to live on your own, and you'll have to take a part-time job too unless you want to end up with a massive debt hanging around your neck. I wish there was another way but there isn't because once you are eighteen there won't be an educational trust to fall back on anymore. I'll give you what I can, of course, but it won't be enough."

Izzie hugged her. "I don't expect you to give me anything. You've already done more for me than a lot of real parents would have done. I'm used to working part-time too, in the stables...so do me a favor and stop talking about university 'cos it's boring. Let's talk about Marcus Lewis. Are you and he an item?"

"Maybe," Jodie flushed pink as they walked towards her car. It was a big and battered Jeep that came with the job and it always looked out of place amongst the sleek cars that lined the school car park on open evenings. Not that Izzie appeared to care. It was Jodie who had the problem. She wanted her sister to have every advantage, and that included not looking out of place at school.

"Brilliant! Wait until I tell all my friends…wow Jodie. I didn't know you had it in you. My sister is going out with Marcus Lewis." Izzie climbed into the car and settled into her seat with a satisfied sigh. Then she saw the expression on Jodie's face.

"Not a good idea?"

"Not a good idea," said Jodie firmly. "Tell them about our trip to London if you must, but leave me out of it…and that goes for everyone at the stables too.

* * *

Marcus arrived early. So early Jodie was still saying goodbye to Buckmaster. Izzie was waiting though. As soon as he drove into the yard she flew out of the house, a rucksack trailing from one hand and a small canvas bag in the other. He raised his eyebrows.

"Is that it?"

She grinned at him. "We believe in travelling light."

"Have you got your music?"

"At the bottom of my rucksack but don't tell Jodie. She thinks this is all about her getting to know you."

"It is," his voice was sharp. "And it's also about both of you getting to know Luke. Listening to you sing is third on my list Izzie."

Looking suitably chastened she opened the rear door and slid into the car. Then she gave a puzzled frown. "Who is Luke?"

He stared at her reflection in the driving mirror. "Jodie hasn't told you?"

76

"If you haven't learned how tight-lipped she is about almost everything by now, then you haven't learned anything about her at all. No, she hasn't told me about Luke. She's never even mentioned his name."

Marcus sighed. Jodie had even more hang-ups than he did. "Luke is my son. He's eleven years old and he's autistic. His autism affects him in lots of ways; for example, he hates meeting new people, so you and Jodie will be a big challenge for him even though he knows he can escape to his own rooms in the apartment whenever he needs to."

She shrugged. "Lots of the kids on the disabled riding program were like that when the started. I take lead rein for one of them, Rosie. We get on really well now but it was ages before she would even look at me."

"Luke has some minor physical disabilities too. He's not very coordinated."

"So do lots of the kids on the program. Surely Jodie's told you about it."

"Mmm. She wants Luke to try it out when we move up here, but I think she'll find she's met her match in him. Luke on a horse surrounded by strangers...no I can't see it."

Izzie laughed. "If that's what you think then you still have an awful lot to learn about my sister."

But Marcus had stopped listening. Following the direction of his gaze she saw Jodie come out of Buckmaster's stable and secure the bolt behind her. Carol, who was taking charge of the riding school for the weekend, was hovering at her shoulder and nodding at the long list of instructions being issued.

Izzie swung her long legs out of the car again. "I'll go and rescue Carol and speed things up a bit. If I don't we'll be here half the morning while Jodie checks and double checks everyone knows what they're doing."

She paused and peered in through the driver's window. "You do know my sister is a control freak don't you?" she said. Then she walked away chuckling.

# Chapter Fourteen

When Jodie finally climbed into the car Marcus deliberately let his eyes travel the length of her body. Then he grinned at her. "What, no riding hat?"

"Sorry to disappoint you." Her cheeks, still pink from her early morning ride, flushed to a deep rose color, and he knew she was remembering his frustration when he fumbled with the straps under her chin the previous morning. He could still remember the little moans and gasps that had been triggered by his kisses once he had managed to drop her hat onto the path beside them. He could still remember, too, the way her body had felt beneath the nubby cotton of her green polo shirt.

He drove slowly out of the yard feeling his frustration building again. Remembering everything about Jodie wasn't difficult. It was the doing something about it that was the problem. They were both too busy and had too many responsibilities. How were they ever going to find enough time to do all the things his libido kept talking about?

He glanced across to where she sat, her fidgeting fingers the only sign she was feeling nervous. Her hair was still in a single plait. Admittedly she had exchanged her jodhpurs for black denims and her polo for a long sleeved T-shirt, but nothing else had changed. She was still wearing a shapeless fleece and sensible boots. Not her usual ones to be sure. The fleece was a nicer color too. It was a rich plum red that complemented her dark hair and olive skin, but it was still shapeless, and it was still a fleece. He wondered if she dressed like that to hide her very tantalizing body from the world, or whether she just wasn't interested in fashion.

He thought of all the women who had fawned over him while he was in California: women who were tanned and toned to within an inch of their lives. Women who wouldn't contemplate leaving the house without full make-up and co-coordinating outfits. He gave a wry smile. What a joke. All those limber beauties with an open invitation in their eyes and he had spent every minute of his spare time thinking about Jodie.

He took one hand off the wheel and briefly rested it on hers. She looked at him for the first time since she climbed into the car and he saw the fear in her eyes. He had learned a lot about her during their transatlantic conversations and he guessed right now she wanted to cancel the whole trip. She wanted to forget all about him and go back to the safe life she had worked so hard to achieve for herself and for Izzie.

He tightened his fingers around hers. "It'll be fine Jodie. We'll be fine."

Then he returned his hands to the wheel and proceeded to regale both his passengers with stories of his trip to California for the rest of the journey. Izzie played ball by asking all the right questions and laughing in all the right places. Jodie, however, was mostly silent, although her lips did curve upwards occasionally. When she and Marcus exchanged glances though, he saw that the fear had faded and been replaced by a tentative promise.

For the moment it was enough.

\* \* \*

It was late morning when he drove down into the secure parking area beneath his London apartment and slotted his car into its accustomed space. Minutes later they were in the elevator climbing to the top floor.

"Coffee first, or cola for the unsophisticated," he announced, ushering them into the square granite and stainless steel kitchen he rarely used. "After that I'll give

79

you the tour and show you where you'll be sleeping."

Izzie dumped her rucksack onto the tiled floor and rushed across to a door that led out onto a small balcony. Pulling it open she stepped outside.

Jodie, however, stood transfixed in the doorway. "I didn't know it would be like this," she whispered, her eyes dark pools of distress.

He abandoned his search for coffee and took her in his arms. He didn't want her to be overwhelmed by his wealthy lifestyle. It wasn't who he was. "It's just an apartment Jodie. It's where I live when I'm in London. I didn't even decorate it or choose the furniture. Someone else did it for me."

She shook her head. "It's not that. It's just...I...it's like travelling back in time. I used to live somewhere like this a long time ago when Izzie was tiny...when my mother and step-dad were still alive. When we still had money." Her voice trailed off as she looked at the array of electronic gadgets on the counter and the state-of-the-art cooker set into the wall.

He tightened his grip. "Money's not everything."

"I know, but it would have been nice for Izzie to have experienced it. By the time she was old enough to notice, everything had gone. She's never known anything but a hand-to-mouth existence. Most of her school clothes are second-hand and she buys all her fashion stuff from charity shops."

"If how she looked when she first came to my trailer is any indication of her general style then I don't think it holds her back," Marcus teased, his sole aim to bring back Jodie's smile.

She obliged, and when he saw the dimple at the corner of her mouth he abandoned the idea of coffee altogether and kissed her instead. He was still kissing her two minutes later when Izzie clattered back into the kitchen.

"Don't mind me," she told them as she grabbed the cola Marcus had taken out of the fridge. Popping the tab, she had a long drink.

"That's better. I was really thirsty. I'll leave you two

80

to get to know one another better shall I, while I go and explore? Is that okay Marcus? I want to find the other balcony, the one that overlooks the river. I can see a corner of it from the kitchen window."

"Help yourself." Marcus waved his hand towards the doorway as he grinned at Jodie. "Your sister is too cute for her own good but she does have some good ideas."

"You mean the 'getting to know one another better' idea?"

He nodded, and then he bent his head and reclaimed her lips.

* * *

They were disturbed by a single loud bark. They stared at one another; their mouths still only a whisper apart.

"Is that Blue?" Jodie asked.

Marcus frowned. "Yes. So it must be Luke too. Mrs Cotton takes Blue for a walk while he's with his physiotherapist, and then they come back together. They're much earlier than I anticipated though."

A loud shout interrupted him. It was followed by a high pitched scream.

"Oh god…he's discovered Izzie. I was going to warn him…give him time to get used to the idea of strangers in the house. Now anything could happen."

Jodie grabbed his hand as he made for the door. "It'll be okay Marcus. Izzie knows how to deal with children who behave like Luke. They will be fine."

He scowled at her as he tried to shake her off. "Luke isn't part of your riding program Jodie. It's going to take more than that to make him behave in a civilized manner."

He pushed open the door as he finished speaking and hurried through the apartment to a large airy sitting room where floor-to-ceiling windows covered an entire wall. One section was open and Izzie was kneeling on the adjoining balcony making a fuss of Blue. A slim, dark-haired boy was standing in the centre of the room. His eyes were tightly shut and he had his hands over his ears.

"No! No! No! NO! NO!" Each time he shouted his voice grew louder.

Standing beside him was a middle-aged woman dressed in black. She was trying to remonstrate with him without success.

Cursing under his breath Marcus hurried forward, his one aim to put a stop to the spectacle in front of them.

Jodie tightened her grip on his hand and pulled him back. "Give her a chance," she said.

As he tried to free himself, Luke paused for breath. Izzie spoke into the silence.

"Hello Luke. I'm Izzie. I'm your Dad's friend."

Luke started shouting again. "No! No! NO!"

She carried on making a fuss of Blue while she waited for him to draw breath again. When he did, she spoke for a second time.

"I'm Blue's friend too. He's really pleased I've come to visit him. Look. He's wagging his tail."

Luke opened his eyes into tiny slits. Then he snapped them shut again and resumed his shouting.

Unable to restrain himself any longer, Marcus finally pulled free of Jodie and grabbed his son's arm, indicating with a nod of his head that the older woman should leave it to him. Turning sharply on her heel she marched past Jodie with an angry scowl on her face.

"Hello Marcus," Izzie acknowledged him without moving her position. "I've just met Luke. He knows you and Blue are my friends. I want him to be my friend too. He might be once he's stopped feeling cross. He's cross because he didn't know I was going to visit him."

Her precise language stopped Marcus in his tracks. Jodie was right. Her sister really did know what she was doing. She was talking to Luke in exactly the same way he had learned to do himself, and she was pausing between each sentence to give him time to compute what she was saying as well. Instead of giving in to his first instinct and leading Luke out of the room, he stared at Izzie's bent head. Then he turned and looked at Jodie. She nodded encouragingly, indicating with a wave of her hand that he should join her on the balcony.

Not entirely sure why he was doing it, he let go of his son and stepped outside. Izzie stood up and smiled at him. Behind him, Luke's shouts grew louder.

"What a fantastic view," she said.

He nodded. Then, with another glance at Jodie, he replied. For the next five minutes they talked about the view, the river, and finally about the birds fluttering amongst the branches of the trees beside the balcony.

"Luke is the one who feeds them," he said. "He spends all his time watching them. I swear he knows every single one by sight."

"Really? Will he tell me about them once he's stopped being cross? Oh, he doesn't need to because I know what that one is. It's a coal tit." Izzie pointed to a small brown bird swinging from a feeder attached to the side of the balcony. "And that one over there is a green finch...and look, there's a robin."

Behind them they heard the drag of feet on parquet as Luke walked across the room and joined them on the balcony. Ignoring him Izzie continued to point at the birds, naming them at random.

"No! No! No!" But this time Luke's voice was quiet. Too intent on putting her right, he forgot she was a stranger and started to tell her the correct names of each of the birds.

* * *

Hours later, with Luke in bed and Izzie sprawled in front of the television in the next room, Marcus sank into a chair opposite Jodie and sighed.

"I'm sorry I shouted at you," he said. "Luke does that to me. Every time he has a meltdown I tell myself to keep calm, but it never works. I was ashamed of myself when I saw how easily you and Izzie handled him. He was only angry with her for a few minutes and he wasn't fazed at all when he met you. I can't remember him ever managing to eat a meal with unfamiliar people before either.

She leaned across and took his hand. "The birds were the key," she told him.

He laughed as he pulled her towards him. When she was comfortably established on his lap he nuzzled her neck, reveling in the softness of her skin and the lemony scent of her shampoo.

"Yes, there was a bit of a bird theme at the dining table wasn't there? But now he's accepted you he'll be fine so long as you're prepared to talk about birds every minute of every day you're here. He's totally obsessed with them. I'm sorry I was angry with you though."

She twisted her head so she could look at him. "Angry is allowed," she said. "As long as we make up afterwards."

"You mean like this," he murmured, skimming his hand down the length of her body. "And like this…and this."

It wasn't until they heard movements in the adjoining room that they pulled apart, but by then Jodie's normally smooth hair was ruffled and her eyes were twin pools of need. Sliding her off his lap and onto the chair, Marcus stood up and held out his hand.

"I haven't even shown you your bedroom yet."

She shook her head. "I can't Marcus. Not here. Not with Izzie and Luke in the apartment."

He smiled at her. "That's not what I meant. I just want you to pick a bedroom. Preferably the one furthest from mine if that's how you feel."

She slipped her hand into his. "You don't mind?"

"Of course I mind. But I'm trying hard to understand."

\* \* \*

Jodie squeezed the tube of toothpaste with a sigh. Staying with Marcus was going to be difficult. The memory of his kisses, the way his hands had set her on fire, the words he'd murmured in her ear, all of those things had left her taut with need. It was a need she had resolutely ignored for the past ten years, concentrating instead on Izzie, and on building up business at the riding school. Now, however, it

84

had come back to bite her big time. She wanted Marcus with a ferocity that almost overwhelmed her. Almost, but not quite. Even while they were kissing she was aware of her sister in the next room, and had been ready to break away from him at the slightest sound.

She stared at her reflection in the mirror and saw that her lips were swollen. Red, and slick with the water she had just used to rinse her teeth, they shouted out her desire. Her eyes were different too. They were darker and more languorous. She couldn't keep her feelings hidden anymore. Marcus had broken down the barrier between her and the outside world, so now her body as well as her emotions was letting her down.

The familiar trill of her cell phone made her jump. Instantly alert she hurried back to the bedroom and grabbed it from the bedside table. Was something wrong at the riding school? Was Buckmaster okay? A hundred things went through her mind until she saw the caller ID. It was Marcus.

"This is getting to be a bit of a habit," he said when she answered.

Even his voice turned her on. She gave a shaky laugh. "As long as it's a habit you don't want to break."

"I don't, but if someone had told me a few months ago I would get most of my romantic kicks via a cell phone, I'd have laughed at them."

"I already said I'm sorry."

"Hey, I'm not calling to make you feel bad. I'm just calling to say goodnight."

"You already said it, ten minutes ago."

"So I did. Well I'm saying it again. Goodnight Jodie."

She smiled into the phone. "Goodnight Marcus."

* * *

She wasn't going to sleep. She knew that. So she rummaged around in her bag for the book she'd thrown in at the last minute, and then climbed into bed. Five minutes later she was still staring at the first page when Izzie came

85

through from the adjoining bedroom.

"I'm sorry Jodie," she said.

"What for?"

"For being here and spoiling your weekend with Marcus. I'm the reason you're not sleeping with him aren't I?

"This is not a conversation I'm going to have with you," Jodie gave up all thought of reading and put the book on the bedside table, next to her cell phone.

"Why not? I'm your sister. That's the sort of things sisters talk about isn't it? You know…who they fancy…what it's like to kiss them."

"Some sisters maybe, but not this one."

Izzie sighed. "I wish Mama hadn't died, so you could be my sister instead of my mother. So you could have a life of your own, without me."

Jodie put out her hand and pulled her down onto the bed beside her. "I wish she hadn't died too, but don't ever say things like that. If you had died in the car crash as well as her then I think my heart really would have broken into tiny pieces."

A solitary tear trickled down Izzie's cheek. "Do you honestly mean that?"

"Of course I do. I wouldn't say it otherwise. And don't worry about Marcus and me. We'll sort things out in our own way. Now are you going back to your own bed or are you getting into mine?"

"Getting into yours if Marcus isn't going to," a second tear followed the first one.

Jodie pushed back the duvet with a shake of her head. "He's not. He's not even going to come into the bedroom, so get in…but stay on your own side of the bed because I need my beauty sleep."

Climbing in, Izzie kissed Jodie on the cheek, threw the pillow onto the floor and then slithered down the bed until she was lying on her stomach with her head turned away. Jodie ruffled her blonde pixie crop as she leaned across to turn off the bedside light.

"Sleep tight," she said. Then she lay on her back and

listened to her sister's breathing.

She had deliberately chosen adjoining bedrooms with a shared bathroom, knowing it would give Izzie the feeling of security she would need to get to sleep. She had anticipated she would want to keep the doors open between them too, had even expected her to come into the bedroom in the morning. What she hadn't anticipated was that she would want to sleep in the same bed.

She frowned. It had been a long time since Izzie had woken up screaming in the middle of almost every night with a terror that could only be soothed if Jodie climbed into bed with her. Nowadays, although she still had bad dreams, she mostly managed to get back to sleep alone. Surely these few days away weren't going to undo everything she had achieved in recent years. On the other hand, it was a good test. If she couldn't manage to sleep in her own bed this weekend when Jodie was with her, then she couldn't contemplate going away to university either. By the time their short break was over at least they would know whether she could cope on her own, or whether she needed to choose a course at a local college so she could carry on living at home.

Turning on her side, she sighed as she contemplated the future. Where did that leave her and Marcus? Would his understanding stretch far enough for him to accept a relationship that included an ever-present Izzie, or would he get fed up with the whole thing and move on? He had Luke to consider, of course, but it wasn't the same. His money bought him a sort of freedom. He could go away for weeks at a time secure in the knowledge that his son's life would continue exactly as usual, whereas she didn't dare leave her sister even for a single night.

# Chapter Fifteen

Marcus got up early the following morning. Knowing Jodie was asleep on the other side of the bedroom wall was driving him to distraction, as was the memory of her kisses. He groaned as he remembered the way she had slipped her hands up under his sweater and pressed them against his chest.

But even as he struggled with his frustration he smiled. At least with Jodie everything was straightforward. What you saw was what you got. When she was angry she scowled. When she was scared her eyes became pitch dark and opaque. When she was happy her laughter triggered that tantalizing dimple at the corner of her mouth. And when she had kissed him yesterday she had been so turned on by his lovemaking he'd had to call on every bit of his willpower not to push her further. Not with Izzie in the adjoining room.

Izzie. What was it with Izzie? Jodie had told him about the car crash and how Izzie had been trapped in the car. She had talked about the paramedics who had tried to resuscitate her mother at the side of the road, and then told him about her own journey home from the other side of the country, and how scared she had been that she was going to lose Izzie as well. There was something she wasn't telling him though. He was sure of it. Something that ate away inside her, the same way the memory of his wife's tragic death ate away inside of him.

He frowned. They were a fine pair, both of them burdened by tragedy. In his case though, it was guilt that had nearly destroyed him; guilt because he hadn't been there when he was most needed. Jodie was different. She had nothing to feel guilty about…or did she? Was it guilt making her so protective of her sister, and if so, what had she done?

\* \* \*

Mrs. Cotton announced she was up by clashing pots and pans together as she began to prepare Luke's breakfast. With a sinking heart Marcus hurried into the kitchen ready to grovel. He knew he should have told her to expect guests for the weekend. He should have checked up on his son's program too. If he had, he would have known about the change to his regular exercise session in the gym, and been ready for the extra stress triggered by the interference to his routine.

"I'm sorry Mrs. C. I didn't mean to take over like I did yesterday. I wasn't thinking straight. I can hardly hear myself think at all when Luke screams like that," he offered as some sort of explanation.

She gave an angry sniff. "Well all I can say is you were lucky. It could have gone on for hours."

"I know. But calming him down was a bit more than luck. Jodie and Izzie have both worked with children like Luke, so they knew how to talk to him."

"Fat lot of good it'll do them the next time, when he refuses to listen," she wasn't prepared to forgive him yet, and he didn't blame her.

For the past six weeks she had been in sole charge of the team of care workers who worked with Luke and looked after him. She had run the apartment like clockwork too; timing it so that the women who came in to clean didn't upset him, and keeping his contact with strangers to a minimum. She had also made sure he was nurtured and fed. Without Mrs. Cotton running Luke's home/school program, life didn't bear thinking about.

"When did you last have a break?" he asked her, determined to make amends somehow.

"Trying to get rid of me now are you?" her Irish lilt,

which was always such a delight to his musical ear, became stronger as emotion took over.

"You know I'm not," he risked sliding an arm around her shoulders. "I couldn't do without you. It's just I doubt you've taken all the days due to you while I've been away so I'm trying to put it right. Surely there's somewhere else you'd rather be this weekend?"

She shook her head. Then she smiled. "Well maybe just for a day. My niece has a new baby I'd like to see."

"So what's keeping you?"

He put his hands on her shoulders when she began to list all the things she had to do before she could leave the apartment. "I can do everything. And Jodie and Izzie will help too. You go and visit your niece Mrs. C. Luke will still be in one piece when you come back."

She looked at him doubtfully. "Well if you're sure…"

"I am, and to prove it I'll finish making his breakfast," he turned her around and pointed her towards the kitchen door.

She didn't take much persuading, and as he watched her go he felt the familiar guilty lurch in the pit of his stomach. From the outside it probably looked as if he was a good father. He made Luke his priority whenever he could, and when he had to go away he always made sure he was well cared for. Money was no object. The people who looked after his son kept to a daily schedule that aimed to minimize his ever-present stress levels. They worked to his strengths, too, by encouraging his reading and his drawing, and they concentrated on improving his coordination. Yet despite all the care and money lavished on his son, Marcus knew he was a failure…as a father…and as a man.

However hard he tried, he couldn't relate to Luke's small successes, to the tiny steps forward Mrs. Cotton took such pride in telling him about. Although he smiled and nodded in all the right places, he couldn't make himself care when he went a whole week without a tantrum, or when he learned a new skill. All he wanted was to have a normal son, one who could kick a ball around, or talk about music, or even share memories about things they'd done

90

together. He wanted Luke to call him Dad and to know what that meant.

With a sigh he turned back to the cooker. What had Mrs. C said - scrambled eggs, two pieces of toast and a glass of orange juice - all to be delivered at precisely eight-o'clock.

* * *

It was two minutes before eight when he carried the laden tray through to the dining room. Luke was sitting at the table drawing a picture of a bird. He ignored Marcus. He ignored Mrs. Cotton too when she came into the room to say goodbye. Without warning something snapped in Marcus.

"Mrs. Cotton said goodbye Luke."

With no indication he'd heard him, his son carefully slotted a brown felt-tip pen back into its place in his coloring box and selected a green one.

The fact he was still holding the tray was the only thing that prevented Marcus from snatching it from his hand and insisting he answer her.

Mrs. Cotton shook her head. Her eyes were full of compassion. "It doesn't matter. He never says goodbye."

Marcus scowled. "Well he should. Good manners aren't much to ask."

"For Luke they are."

As he opened his mouth to reply, Luke returned the green pen to his coloring box and snapped the lid shut. Then he placed it on top of his drawing pad and pushed both of them away from him, clearing a space for his breakfast tray.

Marcus glanced at his watch. It was exactly eight o'clock. "How do you do that?" he asked irritably as he placed the tray in front of him. "How do you always know what time it is?"

Luke stared at him. "Breakfast is at eight o'clock," he said.

Knowing it was the only explanation he was going to

get, Marcus sighed. Luke only dealt in facts so why did he keep expecting a deep philosophical debate. To him eight o'clock meant breakfast. It was part of his routine. He wasn't interested in the whys and wherefores. It was one of the main reasons Marcus found his behavior so frustrating because in many ways he was very bright. It was as if a good fairy had come along, seen how burdened he was with physical and mental disabilities, and tried to compensate by doubling his intelligence quotient. Academically Luke was several years ahead of his age, and his reading speed was off the scale.

Watching him cut up his toast into equal squares, Marcus remembered how Jodie and Izzie had spoken to him. They had both used short, factual sentences, and they had told him what they were going to do before they did it. It was almost as if they had read the same books he had immersed himself in when Luke had first been diagnosed, books long forgotten in the daily grind of frustration. It had worked for them though, so maybe it would work for him. He cast his mind back to the end of yesterday's evening meal, the first one he could remember sharing with his son for a very long time.

Jodie had stood up, pushed her chair in and spoken directly to Luke. What was it she had said? Something about him having to help clear the table because Mrs. Cotton was busy. And Luke had picked up his plate and carried it into the kitchen without complaint.

Trying to mimic Jodie's tone of voice, he spoke directly to his son. "Mrs. Cotton is going out."

"Okay," Luke replied, his mouth full of egg.

"She said goodbye."

Luke raised his eyes until he was looking directly at Mrs. Cotton but he didn't speak.

Marcus took a huge breath in an attempt to crush his frustration. "Say goodbye to her," he said. "Tell her to have a nice day."

There was a long silence while Luke considered what his father had just said and Marcus knew he had pushed him into overload. The 'have a nice day' concept was not

92

something that made any sort of sense to Luke, not unless it was attached to a fact he could relate to. Why did he always forget things like that? It wasn't as if he didn't know how to handle things. He had read enough about Luke's mental challenges, spoken to enough experts, and yet still he got it wrong.

He gave Mrs. Cotton an apologetic shrug as he turned towards the window. She gave a sketchy wave and made for the door. Behind them Luke took another bite of toast.

"Goodbye Mrs. Cotton," he said, his mouth full of crumbs.

* * *

By eight thirty Marcus had cleared away Luke's breakfast dishes and made sure he had all the pens and pencils he needed to continue with his drawing. Satisfied he would remain occupied until it was time for his daily visit to the pool, he returned to the kitchen. He stacked the dirty dishes in the dishwasher and swiped a cloth across the counter top. Then he spooned coffee into the espresso machine and stood listening to the satisfying swoosh of the steam as it was forced through the ground beans.

While he waited he thought about what Luke had just done. Deep down he knew it wouldn't always work like that. When he was engrossed in an activity his son would keep on ignoring him. He would keep on having tantrums too when things didn't go his way. Right now though, those things didn't seem so important. Right now he was experiencing an unexpected sense of satisfaction because for once Luke had actually responded positively to a request.

Pouring himself a coffee he carried the mug over to the window and stared out into the morning. It was bright with sunshine and the sky was blue. He wondered if he should try to persuade Izzie to stay with Luke for an hour or two so he and Jodie could take a walk by the river. Then he saw Jodie and stopped wondering about anything at all.

She was standing on the slice of balcony visible from

93

the kitchen window. It opened out from the bedroom she had chosen, so he had a clear view, and what he could see made his heart beat faster.

Wrapped only in a towel, she was leaning forward slightly as she brushed hair still damp from the shower. The repetitive sweep of her arm had a hypnotic effect. He watched with baited breath as she pulled the brush through it time and time again. Finally satisfied, she flipped her hair back over her shoulders. It settled like a mantle of dark silk almost to her waist.

Unable to drag his eyes away he continued to watch as she tucked the towel more securely around her and tilted her face up to the early morning sun. It sparked blue lights in her hair while a mild breeze dancing through the leaves sent dappled shadows across her bare shoulders. Her eyes were closed and her cheeks were still rosy from the shower. Marcus ached with need. He wanted to go into her bedroom, lock the door behind him, and take her in his arms. He wanted to unwrap her towel and tangle his fingers in her hair. He wanted to…

Izzie interrupted his raised his blood pressure by coming out onto the balcony and standing beside her sister. She said something that made Jodie laugh and as she did so, Marcus saw her turn back into the old Jodie. Gone was the private abandon with which she had greeted the early morning sunshine. Gone, too, were the sensuous movements of her fingers in her hair. In their place was the practical woman whose desire to protect her sister overrode almost every other feeling.

He sighed when she reached behind her and divided her hair into thick skeins. She was going to plait it. Then she would pull on a long-sleeved T-shirt. By the time she left her bedroom the Jodie he had seen on the balcony, the Jodie he could sense when she was kissing him, would have completely disappeared.

# Chapter Sixteen

Marcus stared at Luke. "What do you mean, we're going to the park?"

His son gave him a withering look. Going to the park meant going to the park. What else could it mean?

"It's my fault. I told him we'd go when you and Izzie got back," Jodie took charge of the conversation.

Luke gave a sigh of relief. She seemed to know what his father was talking about, the same as she knew how much he liked to look at the trees swaying in the breeze. She had joined him on the balcony after his swimming session and talked to him about the birds. Then they had had a long discussion about birdseed. Luke knew a lot about that. He knew it was important to give the birds the right mix, a mix that was different in the summer when they had fledglings to feed. They had talked about the trees too. And the different shapes of the leaves. And then the wind had started gusting around the branches making them sway to and fro. When they did, the nice fuzzy feeling he always got when he watched them had started to creep over him. It must have made Jodie feel the same because soon she stopped talking and just sat beside him and watched the trees too.

Now she was talking again though, and quite loudly. She was having an argument with his father. Luke covered up his ears so he couldn't hear them.

"You had no right to promise any such thing," Marcus said. "Luke doesn't go out, period. We've tried it and it doesn't work. He just gets upset and angry, especially when people look at him."

"That's ridiculous.  You can't keep him trapped indoors forever. He has to learn to cope…with people, with situations, with life. You're not doing him any favors by protecting him like this."

"Easy for you to say," Marcus scowled at her. "You don't have to live with his behavior day after day."

"I know," she put a placatory hand on his arm. "But I do know what can be achieved.  I've seen children who wouldn't even look at a horse when they first arrived at the stables, happily riding around without a leading rein within a few months.

"You and your damned horses! That riding program you run doesn't make you a world expert on autistic children you know."

She withdrew her hand and met his scowl with one of her own.  "I didn't say it did, but I do know Luke is worth more than this.  He's a bright boy. He loves nature, loves the sunshine, and yet he only ever experiences them from a concrete balcony.  What sort of life is that?"

"Why do you think I'm moving to somewhere where he will be surrounded by trees, and where he'll have the freedom of a large garden?  It certainly isn't for my own convenience."

"But he'll still be isolated won't he? Come on Marcus. Give him a chance. Come to the park with us.  If Luke has a meltdown then you can blame me, but I don't think he will."

"Because…?"

"Because he told me he gets to choose what he wants to do for two hours after lunch, and today he has chosen to go to the park to see the birds."

Irritated, because he knew she was right, Marcus gave a bad-tempered shrug.  He couldn't remember Luke ever electing to go out before, but nor could he remember the last time he'd been given the option.  Worn down by his son's tantrums and by what appeared to be his genuine terror of new faces and experiences, Marcus had taken the easy way out. Aided and abetted by Mrs. Cotton and his team of care workers, he had devised a way of life that kept

Luke on an even keel. Apart from going down to the pool and gym in the basement he rarely left the apartment, and when he did he mostly travelled in a car with tinted windows. And yet despite all that he now wanted to visit the park.

What had Jodie been up to while he was at the studio? This weekend wasn't panning out as he'd intended it to at all. Despite that early morning glimpse of her on the balcony, he had barely seen Jodie since. Instead, he'd spent the morning putting Izzie through her paces in his studio while Jodie baby-sat his son. He still wasn't sure how it had happened.

Over breakfast he and Izzie had started talking music, a conversation that had somehow ended with him agreeing to take her to the studio while Jodie stayed with Luke.

"You won't have to do much," he had assured her as Izzie went to the bedroom to collect her jacket. "The girl who takes him swimming will be here in a minute. She'll take Luke down to the pool and work with him for an hour or so, and by the time she finishes another care worker will have arrived."

Jodie had smiled up at him, the memory of the kisses they'd shared in her eyes. "Luke and I will be fine. Izzie will be too, once she's visited your studio. Off you go Marcus because the longer you make her wait the bigger the hints will get."

He had laughed at her as he kissed the tip of her nose. "You're probably right. Your sister is rapidly becoming an open book to me. But make sure you take time to relax. Don't let Luke monopolize you, like he did at supper yesterday."

Three hours later, he was faced with a double dilemma. He had to talk to Jodie about Izzie, and he had to take Luke to the park. He wasn't sure which he dreaded most.

* * *

So when are you going to tell me about Izzie?" Jodie asked. They were sitting side by side on a wooden bench

97

while Izzie and Luke explored the hidden space beneath a weeping willow tree whose leaves trailed across the grass. Luke was wearing a green baseball cap with the riding school's motif on the front, and a pair of dark glasses.

Marcus flexed his shoulders. He could feel the panic building. He still couldn't believe such a flimsy disguise was all it had taken to get Luke out of the apartment and into the sunshine. Surely he would reach melt down soon.

Jodie took his hand. "Stop worrying. He's fine…and if something changes then we'll deal with it."

He looked down at their twined fingers. His were long and slim, and tanned by the Californian sun. Jodie's were short in comparison, with square cut, unadorned nails. Two of them were crisscrossed with healing scratches. He traced one of them with his forefinger.

"You're not going to like it."

"Try me," her fingers tightened on his.

"She needs to sing Jodie. And the world needs to hear her. Keeping Izzie away from music is…well I guess I have the same feeling about it as you do about keeping Luke indoors day after day."

Her face suddenly pale, she turned to where Izzie was sitting. She could only see the shadowy shape of her back through the overhanging branches. She could hear her laughter though. She could hear Luke too. His high-pitched chuckles were the same as those of any other child.

Marcus noticed them as well and when Jodie looked at him again she saw his eyes were bright with unshed tears. He gave her a watery smile.

"We're a fine pair aren't we? We both thought we knew what was best for them and we were both wrong."

She didn't trust herself to speak. Instead she just nodded and then gave herself up to the comfort of his embrace as he slipped his arm around her shoulders and pulled her close.

They sat like that until Izzie and Luke reappeared. Neither of them seemed at all fazed by Jodie and Marcus sitting so close together.

"We're going to the aviary," Luke announced.

"But you've already done that," said Marcus, recalling their slow trek around the cages while they listened to Luke's encyclopedic commentary on every bird. By the time they reached the exit his amazement that his son was such an ornithological expert had overridden his initial boredom. When had that happened? When had his interest in the birds that fluttered around the balcony turned into such an all-consuming passion?

Jodie had seen the expression on his face and laughed at him. "You didn't know did you?

He had given her a shamefaced smile. "Is that what you were talking about this morning?"

"Mmm, and birdseed. I didn't know it was possible to talk about birdseed for over an hour until I met Luke."

And now Luke wanted to visit the aviary again. Seeing weeks of daily visits stretching out before him Marcus groaned. Izzie grinned at him.

"We didn't say you were invited. Luke and I are going to see the birds. You two can carry on canoodling. You can even talk about us if you want to," she added.

Marcus chuckled as he watched her lead Luke across the grass towards the aviary. "She's not exactly subtle is she?"

"It's not her strong point, but she is right. We do need to talk about them. You need to finish what you were about to tell me."

He sighed. "You first."

"No. I already had my turn. You know what I think about Luke."

He tightened his grip on her shoulder as he turned her towards him. "Izzie then. I think you should stop worrying about her and let her do what she wants to do, which is to sing. You need to let her go Jodie."

"And what if I can't?" Her voice faltered.

"Then you'll lose her. She needs to sing. If you had come to the studio with us, you would have seen it for yourself. She has a tremendous voice and a real stage presence as well. It will only take a few phone calls to have people queuing up to manage her."

"That's exactly what I was afraid of," Jodie twisted out of his arms and stood up. She looked ready to run away.

He stood up too. "Why are you so frightened? She's almost seventeen for goodness sake. And the fact she was prepared to ignore trespass signs and come looking for me shows how determined she is. I might have refused to see her, refused to help her, but she was prepared to take a chance on that. She was desperate enough to risk making a fool of herself."

"I wish she had made a fool of herself. I wish you had refused to help her," she backed away from him, her face suddenly pale.

"If that's how you feel then I don't understand why you agreed to let me listen to her in the first place. Nor why you encouraged me to take her to the studio this morning. Why did you agree if you don't intend to see it through?"

"I agreed because it would have broken her heart if I'd said no," tears streaked her face. "I hoped that visiting your studio and spending some time with you would be enough for her. I know she has a lovely voice but I didn't realize she was that good. I thought…hoped… this weekend would be a way of getting it out of her system."

The pain that sliced through his heart at her words took his breath away. Was all this for Izzie? Had she only agreed to come to London in the hope that her sister would get over her dream? Then he remembered their kisses and knew he was being unfair. There was more to Jodie than that, however protective she was of Izzie. Gently he took her hand and led her into the hidden green shadows of the weeping willow.

"Tell me what it is that you're so afraid of," he said.

"My mother…our mother, was the Italian soprano Annetta Parisi. You probably remember the stories about her. She was beautiful and talented and had the voice of an angel, and in the end it killed her. I don't want the same thing to happen to Izzie. I couldn't bear it if I lost her Marcus. I just couldn't bear it."

She didn't make any attempt to hide the tears that coursed down her cheeks as she explained. "My mother had me when she was just twenty. My father, who was only a couple of years older, drowned two days before I was born. Apparently he was larking about and although Mamma asked him not to, he climbed onto the parapet of a bridge near the spot where they were picnicking. Unfortunately, he slipped, probably the result of too much wine, and he hit his head as he tumbled into the fast flowing river. Because she was so heavily pregnant my mother wasn't able to help him. Instead she had to sit amongst the remnants of their picnic and watch it happen. My grandmother said she was never the same afterwards, which is not really surprising. And when I was born I looked so much like him she couldn't even bear to be in the same room with me. As soon as she could, she left me with my grandmother and flew to Rome, and then to London to concentrate on her career."

Marcus pulled her towards him and held her tight. It wasn't what Jodie was telling him that was upsetting; it was the way she was telling it. It was just so many facts recited in a monotone. A story she had learned from her grandmother, not one she could remember herself.

For a long moment she gave herself up to his embrace, then she pulled away from him again. "I lived with Nonna, my grandmother, until I was eight years old, and I probably only saw my mother half-a-dozen times in all those years. Then she met someone who was very rich and she married him."

"At around the same time my grandmother became ill. Fortunately for me though, she hung on long enough for Mamma to enter her happy families phase, so when Nonna died she brought me to England to live with her and my new stepfather."

"And that's when Izzie was born."

"Not immediately. There were a couple of years when I was the favored child. They were good times. Mamma was happy again, and I guess I was still young enough to be cute. She treated me like a doll really, dressing me in expensive clothes, sending me to ballet lessons, even trying to teach me to sing. My stepfather gave me whatever I

101

wanted too; and when he saw how much I enjoyed riding, he bought me a horse."

"He didn't stop after Izzie was born either. Although Mamma and I began to fight as soon as my teenage hormones kicked in, he just kept right on spoiling me. He was the one who encouraged me to take up dressage, and he was the one who used to drive me to the events."

"So what went wrong?"

"He died. Everyone in my life dies Marcus."

* * *

In the sudden commotion of Izzie and Luke returning Jodie managed to scrub the tears from her eyes and plant her sunglasses firmly on her nose. Marcus gave her hand a sympathetic squeeze as the youngsters pushed their way through the branches of the weeping willow tree.

"Are you looking for birds too?" Luke asked, his face flushed from the afternoon sunshine.

"Don't be silly," Izzie answered for them. "They wanted to be where nobody else could see them so they could kiss one another."

"But I can see them," he looked mystified.

"Stop it Izzie. Don't confuse him," Jodie warned. Then she turned to Luke, anxious to steer the conversation right away from her love life.

By the time he had finished telling her how the peacock had fanned its tail feathers in an ostentatious display, they were nearly back at the apartment. Marcus, walking behind, watched her and wondered what other dark secrets she was hiding.

He tried to remember what he had read about Annetta Parisi. He had been little more than a child when she had taken the country by storm with her husky voice and her unusual beauty. Of medium height and slim, with the unusual combination of black hair and turquoise blue eyes, she had been an exotic mix of Jodie and Izzie. She had been emotionally fragile though. He remembered that, even though he couldn't remember reading about when or how

102

she had died.

With a sigh he followed Jodie and Luke into the elevator and pressed the button for the penthouse. He knew she would tell him eventually, he just didn't know when it would be, not with Izzie and Luke sharing every minute of their lives.

# Chapter Seventeen

"Luke and I have plans for this evening, so if you two want to go off somewhere together we'll be fine."

Izzie carried on reading the titles of the DVDs displayed on a double shelf next to the television as she spoke. When nobody answered she looked up. Marcus was staring at her. She scowled at him.

"I'm not exactly incapable you know. Besides Mrs. Cotton's back…I saw her coat on the hook inside the door, and there are other people around too, aren't there? A handyman or something, and a care worker."

Marcus shook his head. "Not during the evening. Everyone but Mrs. Cotton leaves at the end of the afternoon, and she's meant to be having a day off."

"Well she can still have one. I can help Luke if he tells me what to do."

Marcus looked over to where Luke was already busy with his colored pencils. He appeared to be entirely indifferent to the conversation taking place behind him. He looked at Jodie. She wasn't listening either and he knew it was because of what he had just told her about Izzie. Seeing the misery in her eyes, he made up his mind.

"Okay, but only if Mrs. Cotton agrees… and you have to promise to call her the minute there's a problem."

"There won't be a problem," Izzie pulled a DVD from the shelf and carried it over to Luke. He glanced at it, nodded, and returned to his drawing. Although she gave Marcus a triumphant grin she didn't make any of her usual wisecracks. Instead she kept her language factual for Luke's benefit.

"We're going to watch DVDs all evening, and we're going to eat one of the lasagnas Mrs. Cotton keeps in the freezer."

* * *

Jodie's only concession to an evening out was to exchange her T-shirt for a cotton blouse. Its high neck was fastened with tiny pearl buttons. Marcus gave a rueful smile. What else had he expected: a slinky sheath dress, full make-up and six-inch heels?

"I've booked a table at Casa Minelli," he told her. "I thought you might appreciate getting back to your roots. It's an old fashioned Italian restaurant which is still run by the entire Minelli family."

She nodded, and when he offered it, she took his hand. She didn't say anything though. Nor did Marcus push her. For the moment it was enough to be strolling together alongside the Thames as the last rays of the sun rippled in red and purple streaks across the water.

It had been years since he had done anything like this. Ever since his wife died...no, longer ago than that...he'd been too busy working or caring for Luke. There had been no time for romance, no time for anything but work and the daily grind of Luke's routine. Now, with Izzie and his son happily established in front of the television, he wondered why. Why hadn't he found time to live a life, and what was it about Jodie that was making him break all his self-imposed rules?

He glanced across at her. She was difficult and obstinate and she had as many hang-ups as he did, and yet he wanted her more than he had ever wanted anyone. And he didn't just want her physically either; he wanted Jodie herself. Every spiky, bad-tempered frown, every burst of anger, every reluctant smile turned his heart over. So, too, did the commonsense she displayed around Luke and the way she was determined to help him. Jodie was everything he wanted...needed...but did she feel the same way about him?

He knew how much she was attracted to him because she was too honest and unsophisticated to hide it, but what about the rest? Now he had told her what he thought she should do about Izzie would she push him away? Would she be able to accept it or would she insist on retreating back into the safe life she'd built for herself and her sister? He gave an inward sigh. With Jodie it was difficult to tell.

* * *

The evening at Casa Minelli's was a revelation. It started when Jodie responded to Signor Minelli's greeting in fluent Italian, and it continued as she debated the finer points of Italian cuisine with him. When they had finally agreed on a menu that included home baked bread, olives, roast pork with pickled walnuts and a selection of vegetables, Marcus grinned at her.

"Do you want to choose the wine as well?"

"I think Signor Minelli already has," she said laughing. "I know you told me it was a family run restaurant Marcus, but I wasn't expecting this. It's wonderful."

Looking around at the old-fashioned décor and the heavy wooden furniture Marcus experienced a sense of satisfaction. It was swiftly followed by an uncomfortable question. Had he been testing Jodie by bringing her here? Well if he had, it had worked. She got it.

"The Minnelli's are the closest thing I have to family," he told her. "My own parents died years ago, long before I made a success of my career, and...well you know about my wife. What you don't know is that she was a Minelli. I met her when I came here for a meal."

It was another test, a more deliberate one this time. Jodie reacted, but not in the way he anticipated.

"So you bring Luke here to eat sometimes."

It made him laugh out loud. "Don't you ever give up? No, I don't bring Luke here but Signor and Signora Minelli do visit him occasionally. Theyare two of the few people he tolerates."

"In which case you should be able to bring him to visit

them too."

Remembering the successful trip to the aviary he reluctantly conceded she might be right. "I guess so. I'm doing a lot of things wrong with Luke aren't I? Seeing him with you and Izzie has shown me how it could be if I tried to be a bit more tolerant."

She smiled at him, her eyes soft with sympathy. "I wouldn't say you're doing a lot of things wrong. In many ways he's a very lucky little boy to have so much care and attention, and anyway we're not exactly experts Marcus. For him to learn to be flexible and cope with other people will take a lot more support than we can give. We can help though."

At her words his heart leapt into his throat. He leaned forward and covered her hand with his own. "Do you really mean that? Are you in this for the long haul?"

She looked at him for a long moment and then she nodded. "You've turned my life upside down. I tried to stay away from you, you know I did, but I couldn't. And now you've thrown me a curve ball by telling me I've got to let Izzie go as well. I should hate you for telling me I must drop all the plans I had for her and help her to toughen up instead...I should hate you for everything but I...can't...I..."

Her voice trailed off as he lifted her hand to his lips, and when he kissed it her sharp intake of breath echoed the surge of desire that flooded his senses. He groaned.

"And I should hate Izzie, and Luke, for making things so difficult for us. How long will it be before we can have a few hours on our own behind locked doors?"

Her frustration matched his own as they stared at one another but then the bread and olives arrived and soon she was conversing in Italian again as Signor Minelli poured wine from a dusty bottle. When he left to look after another customer, she turned to Marcus with a wicked smile.

"Apparently this wine has some aphrodisiac properties should you be in need of them."

The tension broken, he gave a roar of laughter. "If that's the sort of conversation he's been having with you then it's time I brushed up on my almost non-existent Italian. In the meantime, you can tell me why you know so much about the food."

"I already told you I spent the first eight years of my life living with my grandmother in the mountains of Tuscany. What I didn't say is that my best memories are of helping her in the kitchen and then eating the food we cooked. We grew most of our own food as well."

"And reared pigs too I suppose," he said as the spit roast pork arrived, succulent and aromatic.

She nodded. "Mmm. I can remember sitting on a long wooden bench surrounded by aunts and uncles and cousins and eating a meal just like this."

"Do you still see them?"

He saw the sadness in her eyes as she shook her head.

"No. When my grandmother died Mamma lost touch with the rest of her family. I was sad at first but I soon forgot. Instead I threw myself into riding and into being my step-dad's shadow. I adored him, and when he adopted me and I could call myself Jodie Eriksson instead of Jodie Parisi, I was so excited. Even now I still find it hard to believe he died so suddenly and with so many debts."

"What happened?"

She shrugged. "He borrowed too much against his various businesses and there were poor investments as well. Whatever the cause, he left us more or less destitute. Everything had to be sold."

"Including your horse."

"Horses. Yes, those too. And I had to leave the school I loved and go to one where success was measured by how much pupils could drink on a Saturday night."

"Which is why you spend all your money sending Izzie to a private school in a small town well away from the temptations of city life."

She nodded. "Not that I pay for all of it. An educational trust funds most of it. The insurance company set it up when Mamma died but it stops when Izzie reaches eighteen."

"And you were going to go on supporting her at

university."

"Still might." She gave him a defiant look. "I haven't made up my mind about her music yet Marcus. I need to have a long talk with her first."

Signor Minelli interrupted before he could reply, by clearing away their empty plates and proffering the dessert menu. When they both demurred he poured the last of the wine and said he would bring coffee instead.

By the time it arrived they had stopped talking about Izzie, and Marcus was answering Jodie's questions about Luke's mother and explaining her connection to the family who owned the restaurant. He turned to Signor Minelli with a smile.

"I've been telling Jodie about Lucia."

For a moment a shadow darkened the older man's eyes, but then he smiled and spoke to Jodie in Italian. "My niece was very beautiful Signorina but she asked too much of life, so in the end life asked too much of her. She wasn't strong like you. Nor did she have as much love in her eyes as you have for Marcus. My wife and I have been waiting for him to meet someone like you for a very long time."

Before Marcus could ask Jodie about the blush Signor Minelli's words had brought to her cheeks, a plump gray-haired woman approached the table, her face wreathed in smiles. Unlike her husband, who was enjoying talking to Jodie in his native tongue, she spoke in English with a lilting accent. "Marcus, you bad boy. Why have you stayed away for so long?"

Marcus, who had risen to his feet as soon as he saw her, bent down and kissed her affectionately on both cheeks. "If I came as often as you wanted me to I would be several kilos heavier. The meal, as ever, was wonderful."

"Si, si," she dismissed his compliment with a wave of her hand as she turned to Jodie. "My husband says you speak excellent Italian Signorina. He says you know Italian food too. For us, that is the greatest compliment."

* * *

109

By the time they left the restaurant Jodie and Marcus had been plied with Italian liqueur, tiny amoretti cookies and rich dark chocolate. They had also promised to return when Jodie next visited London.

"Now you've committed yourself to Casa Minelli's I never need doubt you again," Marcus teased as they walked towards the river.

She smiled at him. "You didn't need to doubt me anyway. I never say what I don't mean Marcus."

He slipped an arm around her shoulders and pulled her close. "I know you don't and I love you for it. Actually I love everything about you Jodie Eriksson…and if you'll just stop walking for a minute I'll prove exactly how much."

When she raised her face to his he led her deeper into the shadows until they were hidden beneath a tree that drooped its branches towards the river and began to feather kisses across her cheeks to her mouth. Then he started an assault on her lips. After that it was a very long time before either of them uttered a word.

# Chapter Eighteen

Nobody said much on the journey north the following afternoon; Izzie because she was listening to music on her iPod; Jodie because she was worrying about the future; and Marcus because he was as frustrated as hell.

When he and Jodie had arrived back at his apartment at the end of the previous evening, all the lights were on and the television was blaring. Izzie was sprawled across the couch, half asleep. She uncurled her legs and sat up when she saw them.

"Did you have a good time? Where did you go? What did you eat? I want to know everything."

"If that's because you think it will add a bit of color to the story you're going to tell all your friends at school on Monday, then you can forget it. Tell them about the trip if you must, but leave me and Marcus out of it." If Jodie was irritated her sister was waiting up, she didn't show it. Instead she sat down next to her and stared at the television.

"What on earth are you watching?"

"One of those late night chat shows I never get to see at home because we don't have Sky or Cable."

She turned to Marcus with a sigh. "Can you believe it? We must be the only people in the whole country who still only watch the terrestrial channels."

"Don't take any notice of her. She manages to watch plenty on the computer, including stuff I probably wouldn't approve of if I knew about it."

"Chance would be a fine thing, what with homework, the work I do in the stables, and mostly because the computer is on the kitchen table where you can see it."

Forcing a smile, Marcus joined in with the banter. Remembering what Jodie had told him earlier in the evening, he also banished all thought of spending the night with her. In the shadow of the tree beside the river she had matched him kiss for kiss until they were both trembling with a need that had been building for hours. With shaking fingers, he had attempted to undo the pearl buttons at her throat.

"You don't make things easy do you?" he grumbled. "First that damned riding hat, and now these buttons."

He could feel her laughter as she pressed against him. "They're just for decoration," she told him. "It's got a zip down the back."

With a growl of frustration, he turned her around, found the zip and lowered it just enough for him to kiss the soft skin in the angle of her neck. Then he pulled it up again and, wrapping his arms around her, held her still until the pulses beating through them quieted. Only then did he voice his frustration.

"We can't go on like this Jodie. Between us we have two homes plus another one half-built, and yet we never manage to be alone together in any of them for more than a few minutes at a time."

"We might have to go on like this for a while at least," her voice was muffled as she rested her head on his chest. "We can't just get rid of Luke and Izzie. They are part of our lives."

His sigh was heartfelt. "I know, but surely we can have tonight. They must both be asleep by now, and Mrs. Cotton never comes out of her room after ten o'clock."

"If only it were that simple. Izzie will be awake. I know she will. And after she's asked us about our evening she will have a jokey conversation about something or other to cover up the fact she's frightened to death of going to bed on her own."

"But she's not on her own. I know Luke's no help but Mrs. Cotton has been there all evening. I wouldn't have left them otherwise."

Jodie moved away from the shelter of his arms and

112

walked over to where a brick wall flanked the river. Staring at the fractured reflection of the moon in the rippling water she carried on talking.

"It's not that simple. She won't even be able to get ready for bed until I'm there. She slept in my bed last night Marcus, and my guess is she'll want to do the same tonight."

Pulling her back into his arms, Marcus tilted her face towards his so he could look at her. He couldn't hide his astonishment. "But that's ridiculous! How on earth is she going to manage her singing career if she can't even go to sleep without you?"

"That's what I've been trying to tell you ever since we met. Despite being almost seventeen, Izzie is a fragile child underneath all that over-the-top confidence. I'm not even convinced she'll cope with university unless she can get a place close enough to home for her to carry on living with me."

"And in the meantime you're going to continue to put your life on hold," his anger and frustration bubbled to the surface. "You can't do that Jodie, not to yourself...not to us."

"I have to. Her whole life has been blighted by a tragedy I might have been able to prevent if I hadn't insisted on leaving home, so I can't give up on her. Besides there's no one else, so it's not even a choice."

"I'm not asking you to give up on her; far from it. But she can't go on behaving like that. She needs help. She needs a therapist of some sort. I'll make a few phone calls tomorrow to see if I can find someone and then I'll willingly pay for as long as it takes...I..."

Jodie didn't let him finish his sentence. Instead she shook off his arms and glared at him. "We're not a charity case Marcus. Izzie and I managed very well on our own until you came into our lives and turned everything upside down, and we can do it again if we have to."

He glared back at her. "Don't be so damned touchy. It's just money, and I'm not going to apologize for having a lot of it because I've earned every penny. You want to help

113

Luke; fine, go ahead with my blessing. I want to help your sister but unfortunately I can't do something noble and self-sacrificing that will meet with your unqualified approval. All I can do is offer to pay for therapy you can't afford, so if you're going to turn it down because of some warped sense of pride, then go ahead, just don't tell Izzie. If she learns you've refused to accept the help she so obviously needs, and with it her chance to succeed in a career she spends every minute dreaming about, I don't think she'll ever forgive you."

Their standoff lasted a full minute before she shook her head. "I won't turn it down but it still doesn't feel right. I'm not used to taking handouts and I wouldn't take this if it wasn't for Izzie."

He gathered her close again. "It's not a handout. I'm doing it because I love you."

When she tilted her head back to look at him, he smiled at her, relieved he had managed to negotiate his way past her prickly independence. "I'm doing it for Izzie too, of course. I do want to help her, never doubt that; but I also have an ulterior motive. Paying a therapist to get her out of your bed has to be a good investment."

* * *

Now, however, after another frustrating night, he didn't feel quite so sanguine. With his foot hard on the throttle, he brooded over what was likely to happen in the months ahead until his house was complete and he could move north. He would have to spend the bulk of his time in London, with Luke, and there was his work too. The film was almost complete but he would have to make at least one more journey to the States before he started packing. There was all the usual promotional stuff and the lectures he had committed to as well. And while all that was happening Jodie would carry on running her riding school and Izzie would take her exams, and he would be back to late night phone calls and Luke's tantrums.

# Chapter Nineteen

His worst fears realized, Marcus stared out the window of his London penthouse and wondered why his life was such a god-awful mess. With Jodie too busy to take another weekend break, the demands of his work keeping him penned in his London studio, and his responsibilities for Luke keeping him at home, they hadn't seen one another for what seemed like weeks. Even their late night conversations had lost their attraction because they were too full of work and of Izzie and Luke. The excitement of those early transatlantic calls had given way to frustration now he had actually held Jodie in his arms and kissed her. He wasn't interested in prolonging a long distance love affair any more. He wanted her in his house and in his bed and the impossibility of the whole thing was eating away at him.

They should be able to manage an occasional weekend break. Other people did. Other people fitted their lives around love and romance, whereas with him and Jodie everything was topsy-turvy. Izzie had to come first, and Luke. Their own feelings and his increasingly frustrated libido had to fight for a place at the very bottom of the pile.

He had given up trying to explain how he felt to Jodie because she was too busy at work, and too worried about Izzie's future. They had agreed to shelve discussing therapy with her until after her exams. It had seemed a sensible decision at the time but now, with the summer looming and no progress made, he felt powerless. He felt ashamed too. He wished he could care about Luke with the same dedication Jodie had for her sister, but he couldn't.

He supposed he loved Luke but the only time he actually spent with him was when he wanted to make sure his carefully calibrated program was still running smoothly. Once he was sure it was he retreated to his studio and left him to Mrs. Cotton. He knew he behaved like that because Luke didn't do empathy, the same, as he knew his son couldn't help his condition any more than Izzie could help her nightmares, but knowing didn't help.

With a sigh of frustration, he turned away from the window and stared at the piano. He didn't play much when he was in his apartment. Mostly he worked in a studio half-an-hour's drive away if the traffic co-operated, and a lot longer when it didn't. Tonight though, he needed to play. He opened the lid and ran his fingers across the keys. Then he pulled out the piano stool and sat down.

He was still sitting there when Big Ben chimed midnight. As the deep chimes of the Westminster clock echoed across the park he shook his head in momentary confusion. He had been so lost in his music he had forgotten to call Jodie, and he couldn't call her now because she always got up so early it wouldn't be fair to wake her. He went searching for his cell phone and found it on the kitchen counter. There were three missed calls, all of them from Jodie. The last one had been made at eleven o' clock.

With a muttered oath he shoved the phone into his pocket and hurried through to his bedroom.

* * *

When Jodie woke up she felt fine until she remembered Marcus hadn't returned her calls, then she felt sick. Had he finally had enough? If he gave up on her because of Izzie, she wouldn't blame him. Maybe it wasn't that though. Maybe it was all about her because although she'd promised to do it, she still hadn't managed to reorganize her work schedule so she could visit him in London again. Remembering the evening they'd eaten at Casa Minelli and what Signor Minelli had said to her about

116

Marcus needing her, she wondered how she could have been so stupid.

She knew, if she asked her, Carol would willingly hold the fort again. Izzie would love it too. When she wasn't studying she spent all her time talking about Marcus as well as singing along to the music he had recorded for her, telling her it was all he was prepared to do until she had taken her exams.

Throwing back her covers she climbed out of bed and walked across to the window. She would do it. She would find a way somehow, even if she had to work every night for weeks to make up for it.

Automatically she scanned the yard, checking everything was okay. The usual sounds of early morning assailed her; the grunt of the horses, the birds calling to one another, the whisper of leaves rustling in the trees; sounds that would be lost in the general hubbub as soon as the stable boys and girls arrived. This was her favorite time of day. Her hour with Buckmaster was what kept her sane. She couldn't imagine life without him.

She reached for her jodhpurs but before she could pull them on a movement distracted her. Someone was standing amongst the trees behind Buckmaster's stable, someone who must have climbed over the gate because, until she unlocked it, it was the only way anyone could get into the yard.

With no thought for her own safety she hurtled down the stairs barefoot. Wrenching open the front door she pulled an old riding crop from a peg on the wall and brandishing it, ran across the yard. She was ready to fight for her horse, ready to scream blue murder if it came to it. She just hoped if it did that Izzie would wake up because although it took her forever to fall asleep, once she had, very little disturbed her.

Trying hard to stop her voice from trembling, she shouted at the shadow in the trees. "Whatever you're doing, it's trespassing. This is private property and I'll call the police if you don't come out right away."

Marcus came out smiling and holding his hands up in

117

surrender. Jodie took one look at him and burst into tears of fright mixed with relief. "You shouldn't have done that," she sobbed as he gathered her into his arms.

* * *

Much later, over breakfast, they smiled at one another while Izzie scolded them for not waking her up.

"I can't believe I slept through everything," she moaned. "It's like something out of a fairy story…you know, brave princess determined to save her beloved horse only to find out that the intruder is her long lost prince."

"Except I'm not lost," Marcus pointed out.

"You might as well be for all we've seen of you recently. When can we come to London again Marcus?"

"Whenever you like."

"What about next weekend then?"

Jodie shook her head. "Marcus is going to America on Friday, and besides your exams start on the following Monday."

She looked glum. "Two whole weeks of slog but…hey…then it'll all be over and we can visit Marcus and Luke for as long as we like."

"We could if I didn't have a riding school to run," Jodie finished her toast and began to stack the breakfast dishes. Marcus stopped her.

"I'll finish that while you go and do horsey things with Carol."

Izzie stared at them. "You're going to take the day off aren't you? You're going to play hooky while I sit in school being bored to tears because all we're doing is going over everything I know already."

"It's a tough life," agreed Marcus with a grin. "You'll get over it though, and later on you can sing for me. The studio is all but ready now so we can try it out."

Her smile was like the sun coming out. "Deal! Have a good day."

They listened to her feet thumping on the stairs as she went to fetch her books. Then Marcus gave a mock frown.

118

"You heard what the lady said…if we're to have a good day then you need to talk to your assistant manager sooner rather than later."

"I'm going…I'm going," but although Jodie moved swiftly across to the door, she wasn't fast enough to evade Marcus. Nor did she want to. Instead she gave herself up to his kisses, only pulling away when she heard Izzie slam her bedroom door.

* * *

When they eventually walked down the lane from the stables to where Marcus had parked his car, it felt strange. Apart from their evening at Casa Minelli and a few stolen moments when Izzie and Luke were busy, they had spent very little time alone together.

"Where shall we go?" he asked as he opened the passenger door.

"Let's visit your house. I can't see it from the bridleway now all the laurel bushes have been planted, so I don't know how close it is to completion."

He shook his head decisively. "I didn't drive over three hundred miles to drink builder's tea and listen to Bill's long list of complaints. You'll have to come up with something better than that Jodie."

"You could make some real coffee while we're there," she teased, remembering the face he had pulled when he tasted the mug of instant coffee she'd handed him earlier that morning.

He grinned at her. "Not even that can tempt me. How about the Lake District? We can be there in an hour or so but it's still far enough away from anyone we know for me to have you all to myself."

* * *

By mid-morning, arms entwined, they were strolling along the banks of Derwentwater. Smooth as glass, it shimmered in the late spring sunshine. In the distance they

119

could see people in brightly colored life jackets paddling canoes, while closer to the shore a flotilla of ducks squabbled over scraps of bread.

Later, they pulled one another up a wooded slope, leaving the lake behind them as they searched for somewhere to sit and enjoy the spectacular scenery. Long before they found it though, Marcus tumbled Jodie into a grassy hollow that was hidden from view by the green fronds of new fern and the black skeletons of dried heather.

"I thought walking by the lake would be enough, but I was wrong," he told her, supporting his weight with his hands as he leaned over her.

She smiled up at him, her eyes dark as sloes in the shadow of the ferns. He felt his breath hitch in his throat as he claimed her mouth. This wasn't how he'd imagined their first time but he wasn't strong enough to fight it, not when she was so eager and willing and the sun was so warm on his back. With a muttered oath he sat up and pulled his T-shirt over his head.

The touch of Jodie's fingers as she stroked his shoulders was the final straw. He covered her hands, stilling them. "Only if you're sure Jodie. It doesn't have to be like this."

"Yes it does," her voice was soft as she pulled her hands free, sat up, and unbuttoned her polo shirt.

He helped her take it off and then he unhooked her bra, releasing breasts that put his imagination to shame. He didn't touch her though. Instead he removed the band at the end of her plait and gently unwound her hair until it tumbled down her back in blue-black waves.

"I've wanted to do that ever since I first saw you," he whispered, tangling his fingers in the thick skeins and pulling her towards him. He took his time after that, savoring her lips and the soft curves of her body before lying down and lifting her above him so the thick curtain of her hair screened them both from view. Then he took her nipples into his mouth and kissed them from pink to a moist, beckoning red.

Lost to everything around them they didn't hear the

voices until a small black and white dog burst through the ferns and started barking. Ignoring the angry commands of its owner, it darted at them, trying to nip them with its sharp little teeth.

With a muffled exclamation Marcus struck out at it. A lucky blow sent it yelping back to its master, and moments later they heard laughter as a group of hikers speculated about what sort of animal it had disturbed in the undergrowth.

Lying in one another's arms, Jodie and Marcus waited in vain for them to go away. When they heard them settling down to eat the sandwiches they were carrying in their rucksacks, Jodie got an attack of the giggles. Smothering the sound against Marcus' shoulder, she began to hiccup.

With a grin he did the only thing he could think of to stop her. He wrapped his arms around her and started kissing her again, and he carried on kissing her right through the sandwiches and the apples that followed. He didn't stop until the last sandwich bag had been collected and the dog had been called to heel. He didn't stop until the voices faded into the distance and they were alone again, but by then it was too late. The sun had gone in, rain clouds were threatening, and Jodie was shivering.

With a wry smile he helped her into her clothes and handed back the hair band he'd stuffed into his pocket. Then he pulled on his own T-shirt while she swiftly pleated her hair into a neat plait.

As they retraced their steps back to the car park he slipped his arm around her shoulders. "Sorry Jodie. I guess making love to you amongst the ferns wasn't one of my best ideas."

Snuggling against him for warmth, she gave a soft laugh. "I wouldn't say that...after all we did discover a very effective cure for hiccups."

# Chapter Twenty

Later, sitting opposite to one another at a table in an ancient waterside inn, they ate local venison and toffee pudding, and laughed at what had so nearly happened to them.

"The headlines wouldn't have done your career much good," Jodie teased as she scooped up the last of her dessert.

"Which one? The one that says 'Composer caught in flagrante in ferns' or the one that says 'the musician caught making love to a beautiful woman protested that he couldn't stop himself because she's the love of his life.'

"The second one," Jodie's voice was barely a whisper as she reached for his hand.

Their fingers clasped, they waited while the waitress cleared the table and took their order for some freshly percolated coffee. Once they were alone again he leaned forward and brushed an errant strand of hair away from Jodie's face. "You do know I mean it, don't you?"

She nodded, but her eyes were full of pain and she pulled her pulled hand free as the waitress returned. "We needed today Marcus…but that's all it is…a day. One day and then it's work again, and Izzie and Luke, and fighting to find enough time to sleep."

He stirred his coffee thoughtfully. "It wouldn't be like that if you married me…well the fighting to find enough time to sleep might be if you were sleeping in my bed…but everything else would be better. Izzie and Luke would soon accept their new life, and I would be able to look after you instead of watching you work your fingers to the bone."

When he looked at her, her eyes were brimming with unshed tears. He took her hand again. "Is that a yes?"

She shook her head. "It's a no. I love you and I want to keep seeing you, but I can't marry you. I can't give up my home and my job at the riding school either. It's just...it's not an option."

"Okay, I accept it's probably too soon to think about it now, but later, when my house is finished and Luke and I are settled, will you think about it then? I'll even have a stable built for Buckmaster...and before you shout at me, I'm not trying to buy you. I know you come as a package...you, Izzie and that damned horse."

"It's not that. It's me," she interrupted him with a shake of her head. "I can't marry you Marcus. Not now. Not ever."

"But why?"

"Because I'll never be able to trust you. My mother trusted people and they all let her down; my father, my stepfather, the man she was living with when she died, me...I let her down too." The tears had spilled over now. She scrubbed at her face with a crumpled paper napkin and blew her nose. Then she pushed back her chair and went to the restroom.

Marcus had settled the bill by the time she returned and was waiting for her by the open door. He wasn't looking at the picturesque scene in front of him though. Instead he was trying, unsuccessfully, to curb his anger. As soon as she joined him he pulled her outside and marched her across to the car. Opening the passenger door, he waited for her to climb in and then slammed it shut.

"You can't live your life like that," he said as he slid into the driver's seat. "I'm not the men your mother knew and you're not your mother. You're strong Jodie, and brave, and determined. Surely you don't think I would do anything to destroy that. I just want to love you and share my life with you. I didn't think I'd ever feel this way again, but I do. When Lucia died I lost my faith in the whole of the human race for a while, but I got over it, so why can't you."

She hunched away from him, trying to escape from the hurt and anger in his voice, and when she finally answered him she was crying again. "I just can't. I know I'm being unfair to you and I'm sorry. I do love you and I'll do anything you want except that. I'll readjust my work, delegate things, find more time for you...for us...but I won't give up my job, and I won't marry you."

With a muttered exclamation he pulled her towards him and buried his face in her hair. He wanted to be angry with her. He wanted to shake some sense into her, but he couldn't because he recognized her pain. He'd had enough therapy after his wife's suicide to know Jodie's fears were irrational. What he didn't know was what he could do about them.

He tried again. "Look, I know it's too soon to think about marriage so I promise not to mention it again if you promise to stop crying. Three times is more than enough for one day."

She lifted her head and gave him a watery smile. "If you told Izzie how often you've seen me cry she wouldn't believe you. She's never seen me cry, not once."

He stared at her in disbelief as he remembered the histrionics that had been part and parcel of his marriage to Lucia. "Never?"

She shook her head. "I cried a lot when my mother died but after that something seemed to dry up inside me and I never cried again until I met you."

"You still haven't told me exactly how she died."

"She was driving too fast, late at night, when she plowed into the back of a parked truck. She was killed outright. Izzie should have been too, except she was lying down, asleep on the back seat, so she missed being crushed by the wreckage."

"But I thought you said she was in a terrible state when you eventually got to her."

"She was, but it wasn't physical. She walked away from the crash without a scratch. It was the shock that unhinged her. The shock of waking up in a tangled mass of metal and seeing her mother dying in front of her. It's why

124

she has such trouble sleeping."

A car horn blared loudly behind them. Glancing in the mirror Marcus saw the driver of a large black car waiting for his parking space. With an apologetic wave he buckled his seat belt and drove out of the car park. He continued for several miles until he saw a wooded clearing beside a different lake. Indicating, he pulled in and cut the engine; then he turned and looked at Jodie.

"What is it you're not telling me?"

Panic washed across her face. "How do you know?"

He sighed. "I know because I love you, and I know because you're an open book. Do you have any idea how expressive your face is? You wouldn't know how to hide your feelings from me if your life depended on it."

When she didn't answer, he squeezed her hand. "It's not a bad thing Jodie. I love that you don't hide how you feel about me. I love that you aren't coy about wanting to sleep with me. What I don't like though, is your need to hide something from me. If you really feel you can't trust me then I'm not sure we can build a future together after all."

The silence between them lasted for so long that in the end Marcus got out of the car and walked across the pebbled beach that fringed the lake. The weather had deteriorated into lowering clouds and a wind was whipping up choppy waves. The grayness matched his mood. He turned and began to trudge along the footpath skirting the gloomy stretch of water.

He hadn't gone very far when Jodie slipped her hand into his. She was out of breath from running and her face was rosy with exertion, but her eyes were dark pools of pain.

"I didn't mean to shut you out Marcus...it's just...it's something I've never discussed with anyone before, not even Izzie because she's too young, but mainly because there has never been anyone else to talk to I guess. My mother's so-called friends, the ones who fawned all over her when my stepfather was alive and she had lots of money, had all given up on her by the time she died. I had too, and I can't forgive myself for behaving as I did. If I'd stayed with her instead of taking a job in a training stable several hundred miles away in the hope I could re-establish my dressage career, I might have been able to stop her chasing across the countryside on a fool's errand."

He wrapped his arms around her, and waited. He knew all about not being there when someone you loved needed you.

"She was pregnant you see. Pregnant with a baby nobody wanted. She went back to singing after my stepfather died. I think it was that or starve. People had forgotten her by then of course, so she only performed in local clubs and bars while I babysat Izzie, but we were fine…until she met Sean. He told her he was an agent but I don't think he was, not really. He was just a chancer who saw an opportunity and sweet-talked her into believing him. He had grand plans for her until she became pregnant."

"Although he was the baby's father, as soon as he saw how her pregnancy was going to affect her career, he left. Her crazy late night trip was because someone at the club where she was singing told her they had seen him and she was trying to find him. I guess she wanted to persuade him to come back to her."

"So when she died, the baby died too, letting him off scot free?"

"No. That's the bit I've never told anyone. The baby was born at the side of the road. A doctor cut her out of my mother's dead body and rushed her to the nearest hospital. I don't know how much Izzie saw because nobody knew she was in the car until the breakdown truck arrived to tow it away and a policeman found her hiding under a blanket on the floor. She was in such a state of shock it was days before she spoke and when she did she refused to say anything about the crash. She still won't talk about it now.

"What happened to the baby?"

"That's the thing…I don't know. Somewhere on this planet I have another sister but I can't find her. I tried. God knows I tried. But nobody would ever tell me anything."

126

The wind blew flurries of rain across the lake as she finished speaking. Feeling her shiver, Marcus turned around so they could retrace their steps. "Come on, you can tell me the rest in the car."

"There's not much more to tell. Social Services had the baby fostered and then adopted. They wouldn't even let me see her, and because I was busy fighting for Izzie I didn't question their decision. It was only after I'd found a home for both of us that I had the time to think about her, and by then it was too late. She had vanished from our lives.

They reached the car as she finished speaking and as soon as they were inside he pulled her into his arms. He was emotionally drained by everything she had just told him; unable to fathom how she had retained her capacity to love after being let down so many times. He was beginning to understand, too, why she had a problem with trust, and he wished he could do something about it.

I don't know what to say Jodie…except that I want you to marry me even more than I did an hour ago."

When she started to react, he took her face in his hands and kissed her. "No, don't say anything. That wasn't a proposal; it was a declaration of intent. One day you'll marry me Jodie Eriksson but until then I'll be content with this…and this…and this…"

\* \* \*

By the time they drove into the stable yard Marcus' and Jodie's energy levels were at rock bottom. They had shared too many confidences and suffered too many frustrations to want to do more than sit quietly together with a glass of wine. Izzie, however, hadn't forgotten their promise. She came hurtling out the house before Marcus killed the engine. She was clutching a sheaf of music.

"What kept you? I thought you'd be here when I got back from school."

He forced a smile. "Hop in. You can be the first one to christen my studio."

# Chapter Twenty-one

Jodie stared out the window as she rinsed the breakfast dishes and wondered what Marcus was doing. She was fed up with late night telephone conversations, especially the ones they'd been having recently, the ones that were a verbal assault on her overheated senses. The ones that kept her awake long after she had cut the call and turned off her bedside light.

Hearing Izzie moving around upstairs she gave a wry smile. At least someone was happy and fulfilled. Her sister had grown up over the past few months. Ever since she had finished her exams she had been focused in a way Jodie had never seen before. When she wasn't immersed in her music she spent hours working with the private therapist Marcus had found for her, and it was all beginning to pay off. Her voice was stronger, her confidence was growing; and in recent weeks, although she still used a night-light, she had also begun to close her bedroom door.

Remembering the uncomfortable end of year meeting with Izzie's teacher she sighed. She was fed up with the constant stream of advice she had received ever since she had agreed to let her leave school. Nobody understood, but then they hadn't seen Izzie perform. Although she was still desperately afraid for the future, she had known she had no choice the moment her sister climbed onto the small stage in Marcus' studio and opened her mouth. Reluctantly she had been forced to accept that Izzie was born to sing in the same way she, herself, had been born to ride.

She knew Marcus had been surprised by how quickly she had abandoned her long cherished ambition for Izzie to attend university. What he didn't understand was that all the knocks she had received in her own life had taught her to be a realist, and it was this that had helped her to accept that Izzie was going to sing, the same as it had made her stop resisting the overwhelming feelings she had for Marcus.

A blast of music interrupted her thoughts as Izzie plugged her iPod into the state of the art docking station Marcus had given her despite Jodie's protests. She was used to the constant background noise by now and was surprised by how much it comforted her. It reminded her of one of the best parts of her childhood when recordings of her mother's music played while her grandmother told her stories about the beautiful woman she only knew through photographs.

Now though, it brought her back to the here and now with a start. She glanced at her watch. It was late. Buckmaster would become restless if she didn't saddle him up soon, and she would be late for her first lesson as well.

Pulling on her riding boots and grabbing her fleece she hurried out into the yard. It was already bustling with activity as stable boys and girls prepared the horses for the day. She waved at them as she made her way to Buckmaster's stable.

He greeted her with a snort of annoyance. She laughed as she offered him a carrot. "I know I'm late Bucky but so would you be if you had as much going on in your head as me."

\* \* \*

Later, trotting along the lane leading to the bridleway her heart leapt when she saw a huge pantechnicon turning into the driveway leading to Marcus' house. At last the months of waiting were over. Sensing her change of mood, Buckmaster slowed down. She dug her heels into his flanks.

"He won't be here yet Bucky and when he does arrive you won't be seeing much of him, not until Luke is ready

129

to visit us."

With a toss of his head the big chestnut gelding moved across to the bridleway and waited for her to unlock the gate. Sliding off his back she slotted the key in the padlock, pushed open the gate and led him through, wondering, as she did so, how long it would take her to persuade Luke to sit on a horse.

She thought of the frowning, dark haired boy she had last seen in London, too intent on his drawing to say goodbye to her and Izzie, and wondered if he would remember them. Despite the success of their visit they hadn't managed another one, partly because summer was Jodie's busiest time at the riding school but mainly because Marcus had had to return to California twice more in the past three months. This meant surviving on a few snatched meetings when he found the time to travel north to visit his new house, or to work with Izzie. Remembering the frustration that shadowed every visit Jodie sighed. Then her face cleared. Soon it was going to change. In the meantime, it was phone calls or nothing.

\* \* \*

Izzie shouted down from the bedroom window as Buckmaster trotted back into the yard. "Marcus called. He says Luke's thrown a wobbly so it could be hours before they arrive."

"I very much doubt he put it exactly like that," Jodie frowned up at her sister as she took in the implication of the message.

"Well no, but that's what he meant isn't it?"

"Maybe, but you could be kinder about it."

"Telling it as it is, isn't unkind Jodie. Nor is saying that Marcus doesn't have the first idea how to handle him."

"You know that after spending one weekend with him and Luke do you?"

"Yes. I love Marcus, you know I do, but I still don't rate his parenting skills. He'd rather avoid trouble and embarrassment than challenge Luke, and you know it isn't helping him. Do you realize he's never even taken him back to the park to see the birds? When I asked him why, he just shrugged and said he hadn't had time."

"Well maybe he hasn't. And he's anxious to protect him from the Press too don't forget." Jodie's instinctive defense of Marcus warred with her feelings. Izzie was right. Despite agreeing that he wasn't doing enough to help Luke accept other people, he hadn't changed anything. Luke was still bound by his routine. Not for the first time she wondered how he really felt about his son.

She ended the conversation by leading Buckmaster back into his stable but as she began to unsaddle him she felt a stab of guilt. She and Izzie had taken up so much of Marcus' time in recent months that there had been little left for Luke, and she felt uneasy about it.

Every time she tried to discuss it though, Marcus had headed her off by insisting Luke was well looked after and that things would change once they moved. She hoped he meant it. At least he had agreed to let him try the riding program although without any real interest, and she knew he wasn't expecting much success. Well there was only one way to deal with that. She was going to prove him wrong.

Satisfied Buckmaster was settled, she left him happily munching hay and hurried across to the office to check her schedule for the day. Carol was already sitting at the desk, tapping figures into the computer. She looked up with a frown.

"You look worried. Anything I can do?"

"Yes, you can tell me which is the best horse for a boy who is a complete novice and who is likely to have a meltdown if something upsets him?"

\* \* \*

"He's so much worse than I expected that I'm beginning to wonder if I've done the right thing after all," Marcus sounded tired and despondent as he described his journey north.

Jodie listened patiently as he told her how it had taken

him and Mrs. Cotton more than two hours to persuade Luke to leave the apartment, and how he had sobbed and screamed for half the journey.

"I thought he understood about the move. I thought he was ready for the journey and so did Mrs. Cotton, but we were wrong. The noises he made were heartbreaking Jodie. It felt like I was torturing him."

"What upset him? Surely it wasn't the car because he's used to being driven."

"He kept saying he wanted his pencils and then shouting something about the birds. It didn't matter how often I told him there were lots of birds where we were going, he just kept on crying."

"Did you ask him why he was so cross?"

"He wasn't cross Jodie. He was upset."

"Isn't that the same thing with Luke?"

"No it's not. I told you, he kept on crying whatever we said to him. I guess he just didn't want to leave the apartment. As it's the only home he's ever known I suppose I should have expected it."

Hearing the irritation in his voice Jodie changed the subject. Now was not the moment to challenge him. There would be plenty of time later to find out what had really upset Luke. In the meantime, Marcus needed her support.

By the time they cut the call twenty minutes later she had agreed she and Izzie would visit him and Luke at the end of the following afternoon. She sighed as she switched off the bedside light and slid down under the duvet. Marcus might have moved to the village but it was very far from the end of their difficulties. Now, and for the foreseeable future, they would have Izzie and Luke to cope with on a daily basis.

Staring into the darkness she recalled everything she had learned about autism over the years and wondered again what was actually at the bottom of Luke's tantrum. Whatever it was, she was quite sure it had little to do with moving north and everything to do with his precious birds. She thought about the rigid routine of his days and frowned. Izzie was right. Marcus rarely challenged Luke.

Instead he did everything he could to avoid trouble by letting him dictate exactly how he wished to spend each minute of every day, and she knew it was wrong. If Luke was ever going to gain some sort of independence he would have to learn how to fit in with other people.

* * *

When Marcus opened the door the following afternoon Jodie was shocked by his appearance. The past couple of weeks had taken their toll, stripping him of weight he didn't have to spare, and bleaching his tan skin to a sallow yellow. His smile was the same though, and so was his kiss as he pulled her into his arms.

Izzie squeezed past them with a grin. "I'll go and find Luke while you two get to know one another all over again.

Too late, Marcus tried to stop her. "Not a good idea Izzie – he's being difficult today."

She waved away his concern as she disappeared into the house.

Jodie slipped her hand into his. "Don't worry. She's brought him some books about birds. She knows what she's doing."

"Well I'm glad someone does." He tightened his grip on her shoulders as he stared down at her. "I've never seen him like this. What am I going to do Jodie?"

"You're going to leave him to Izzie and show me around your new home."

"That simple?"

"That simple," she reached up and kissed him.

His answering smile wiped the tiredness from his face. "In that case let's start with the bedroom."

"Let's not. I want a properly conducted tour with coffee at the end of it."

"Spoil sport. Come on then. You might even like it enough to want to move in."

* * *

Apart from a couple of empty bookcases and a few boxes waiting to be unpacked in the sitting room, the house looked remarkably lived in. It also looked exactly like his London apartment. There were the same pictures on the walls, and the bowls and various artifacts he had picked up on his travels were displayed on the same shelves and tables. He smiled when he saw the surprised expression on her face.

"It's that money thing again Jodie. The one you disapprove of. A team of people has been sorting everything out for days. You know how Luke is about strangers so they did it before we arrived. They drew up a plan of the apartment and then replicated it as best they could…not that it seems to have helped."

She frowned as she followed him into the kitchen. Keeping everything exactly the same was not going to help Luke. He needed to experience new things…he needed to learn to cope with people. She was still wondering how best to talk to Marcus about it when a stack of Luke's drawings on the kitchen counter distracted her.

She picked one up and examined it. It was a lifelike picture of a blue tit. Underneath was another one with something that at first glance looked like a series of black scrawls on white paper but which, on closer inspection, proved to be a detailed drawing of a vast number of birds flying in the V shape of a migrating formation.

"Marcus…this is amazing!"

"So it should be. He never does anything else but draw."

"No, it's more than that. Look at what he's done," she held the pieces of paper out to him.

He barely glanced at them as he searched for mugs and spoons in the new kitchen. She stared at him as the truth dawned. He didn't believe in Luke. He didn't believe his son was capable of achieving anything. Instead of engaging with him, he protected him. Instead of giving him the sort of choices other parents gave their children. he imposed the sort of routine he knew would keep him occupied and calm. He didn't give him any challenges.

"I'm going to say hello to Luke while you make the coffee." She picked up the stack of drawings and walked out of the kitchen before he could reply. Marcus sighed. If she'd decided to take Luke under her wing as well then they were never going to find time to be alone.

* * *

When he carried the coffee into Luke's sitting room he expected to find his son still sprawled across the beanbag he had refused to leave ever since they arrived. Instead, he was sitting at the table showing his drawings to Jodie while Izzie slouched on the beanbag making a fuss of Blue. For a brief moment his heart contracted. To an outside observer it would look like a normal family scene. Only those on the inside knew about the psychological challenges they all faced.

Jodie smiled her thanks as he placed a mug of coffee at her elbow. "Luke has been telling me about his drawings. He's been studying the migration patterns of birds leaving the country before winter sets in. He's even plotted a chart showing their destinations."

Marcus bent and scratched Blue's ear so Jodie wouldn't see his irritation. He didn't want her to spend their precious time together pandering to Luke. His son had more than enough attention from his team of care workers. Jodie didn't need to get involved, not when she was so busy worrying about Izzie, as well as working her fingers to the bone at the riding school.

As if she knew what he was thinking, she got up from the table and carried her coffee across to the couch. He sat down beside her and shook his head. "I know you want to help but it's not worth it. Luke likes it best when he's left alone to work on his drawings."

He spoke softly, his voice full of regret, and when Jodie turned to look at him his eyes were full of a weary resignation. With difficulty she held onto her temper because she knew it wasn't fair to criticize him when she had only spent a few hours with Luke whereas he had been

135

living with him for eleven years. With an effort she slipped her hand into his.

"I need to spend time with him now you've moved though, and he needs to spend time with Izzie too. We can't just ignore him Marcus."

He squeezed her fingers. "I know, and I'm grateful you want to, but don't expect much in return. You and Izzie have been lucky today because he's already worn himself out with his tantrums. It won't always be like this so you had better prepare yourselves."

She stared at him for a moment. Then, realizing he was tired and irritable and trying hard not to show it, she leaned forward and kissed his cheek. He slipped his arm around her shoulders and pulled her close, burying his face in her hair.

"I so needed to see you. The past few weeks have been impossible. When Luke wasn't playing up, the people in California were on the phone demanding more and more of my time, and if it wasn't them it was the removal people or the builders."

Jodie snuggled closer as she listened, wishing she could have been there for him instead of living so far away. Still, all that was over now. She might not be prepared to marry him but it wasn't going to stop her being with him as much as she possibly could. Nor was she going to give up on Luke whatever Marcus said, but now was not the time to tell him that.

* * *

The rest of the afternoon and evening were uneventful. At seven-thirty Mrs. Cotton took Luke away, glad he was ready to slot back into his bedtime routine.

"I don't know what you did, but I'm very grateful," she said to Jodie and Izzie as she left the room trailing Luke behind her.

"How did you persuade her to move north with you when all her family live in London?" Izzie said as the door closed.

136

"I increased her salary...anyway how do you know where her family live?"

"I asked her. She doesn't seem too keen about being here Marcus. Do you think she'll stay or will you just have to keep throwing money at her?"

"That's none of your business," Jodie exclaimed, horrified by her sister's questions, but Marcus just shook his head.

"She's right Jodie. I do keep throwing money at her but I happen to think she deserves very penny of it because looking after Luke day in and day out is not exactly fun."

Izzie didn't let up. "It's not just her though, is it? There are all those other people who care for him."

"True, but Mrs. Cotton is the key. She manages his program, helps to keep him calm by sticking to his routine, and organizes the daily, weekly and monthly Rota. Without her my life wouldn't be worth living, and nor would Luke's."

"What about when she's had enough and wants to move back near her family? What will you do then?"

"I guess I'll try to get her to change her mind again. Now, can we talk about something else please? I've spent quite enough time thinking about Luke today."

"Fine by me. What are we having for supper?"

He gave a relieved smile. "How about pizza? The local takeaway stuffed a flyer in the mailbox. I think I put it on the hall table. See if you can find it and order something for all of us."

Jodie shook her head in disgust as Izzie left the room. "Sorry Marcus. She seems to think she can say whatever she likes to you. Normally she's a bit more circumspect."

"Don't worry about it. She's had to take a lot of criticism from me during her music sessions so I guess she thinks she can dish it out as well."

"But it's not the same."

"Maybe not, but she needs to be able to stand on her own feet once she starts touring so don't stop her speaking her mind. It's what's going to protect her later on."

"I hope you're right because I still don't like thinking

about it. I'll be a mess when she goes Marcus, you know that don't you?"

He pulled her closer. "Mmm…and I'll be around to pick up the pieces."

She tilted her face up to his. "Promise?"

"I promise, but only if you forget about Luke and Izzie and concentrate on me until the pizza arrives."

# Chapter Twenty-two

Now Marcus had officially moved in, Izzie spent most of her time in his studio, sometimes working with him and the other musicians who occasionally joined him, but mostly working on her own as she practiced everything he told her to. She started writing music as well, making up for her lack of formal training by using the computer program he downloaded for her. Marcus nodded approvingly whenever he found time to go into the studio, which wasn't often during his first few weeks in his new home. Instead he spent most of his time tying up loose ends with his site manager or taking long phone calls from California before making equally long phone calls to his agent.

Jodie was patient. She visited every day; made sure she was available for the occasional evening meal they managed to fit into their busy schedules; and was in apparent agreement with everything he told her. Soothed by her undemanding support and by the fact that at last they could see one another almost every day, even if sleeping together was still a distant possibility, Marcus took his eye off the ball. Hopeful that Luke would soon settle sufficiently for Mrs. Cotton to resume her day-to-day management of his program without any input from him, and equally hopeful he would soon be able to make Jodie see sense and move in with him, he forgot how persistent she could be until he returned from another week in America.

The first thing he noticed when he got out of the car and stretched the kinks from his back were the bird feeders hanging in the trees. When he rather shamefacedly thanked Mrs. Cotton for buying them, knowing he should have remembered how important they were to Luke and bought them himself, he was surprised to discover Jodie was responsible. Frowning slightly, he went in search of his son. As usual, he was drawing, but, unusually, he was sitting outside on the terrace while he did so instead of at his usual table by the window. His cheeks were pink as if he'd spent a lot of time outdoors in recent days. He was wearing a child's version of an only too familiar green fleece as well. And his cap was the one Izzie had given him the day they went to the park.

Wondering how best to find out what was going on, he pulled out a chair and sat down. Luke ignored him. He was far too busy shading the undersides of the leaves on the tree he was drawing. Marcus watched him, surprised by the speed of his hand as it flew across the page. He wished Luke could apply that level of skill and concentration to something more useful than drawing birds and trees but he knew it was too much to ask. He was good though. Jodie was right. Even the bird feeder hanging from a twiggy branch was drawn in exquisite detail, and the tiny blue tit hanging upside down as it pecked at the seeds inside was so lifelike it almost looked as if it were moving.

"I like your picture," he spoke slowly, wondering how best to bring up the subject of Jodie and the birdfeeders. Luke preempted him by offering some unexpected information.

"It's for Jodie," he said, swiftly adding another bird as he spoke.

Glancing back at the tree Marcus saw that another bird had joined the first one and that Luke was drawing the tree in live time. It wasn't just a cleverly executed sketch; it was a narrative of what was happening in front of him.

"It's very good. Do you always draw like this or do you sometimes just remember things and draw them later?"

From Luke's non-reaction he knew he wasn't going to get an answer to something that was probably self-evident to his son so, after a brief pause, he tried another tack.

"When are you going to give it to Jodie?"

"At six o'clock when she brings Bucky."

"She's bringing Buckmaster here? How often does she do that Luke?"

"At six o'clock. She always brings him at six o'clock."

Marcus glanced at his watch. It was five-thirty. He had driven north as soon as he could, anxious to be back in time to see Jodie before bed. Now it seemed as if he had a rival.

* * *

Jodie leaned down from Buckmaster's saddle and pressed the entry phone. She was expecting Mrs. Cotton to pick up, so when Marcus answered she was surprised. He'd said he might be late and she had already reconciled herself to one of his midnight phone calls.

"It's Jodie, Marcus. I wasn't expecting you to be back so soon," she could already feel the tingle of attraction she felt every time she heard his voice.

"So I gather," his response was cool as he pressed the switch that opened the gates.

She frowned. Now what? He had been moody ever since the move. Part of it, she knew, was because despite only living two miles apart, they still rarely managed to spend much time alone. This was something more though, and for some indefinable reason she had a feeling it was about Luke and her visits with Buckmaster. Well he could go hang if that was what it was all about because he had promised she could try to introduce him to the riding program, so that was what she was doing. With a sigh she guided Buckmaster through the gates and set off down the driveway as they closed behind them. Whatever his problem he would have to deal with it because she wasn't going to give up on Luke, and she wasn't going to let Marcus give up on him either.

He met her at the end of the drive with his arms folded across his chest and a scowl on his face. "When were you going to tell me about Luke?"

She stared at him. "If you mean the six o'clock visit I make each evening I'm not sure it has anything to do with you?"

141

"So my being his father counts for nothing does it?"

"Don't be silly, of course it does, but I'm not going to take him anywhere if that's what you're worried about. I'm just getting him used to the idea of a horse…and before you say anything else, I cleared it with Mrs. Cotton and she's built it into his activity program. She even seems to think it might be a good idea, unlike his father."

They locked eyes for what seemed an eternity, and then what might have been the trace of an apologetic smile flitted across Marcus's face.

"I might have known going to California was a bad idea. Not only did I miss you like crazy but I left the way open for you to start indoctrinating my son into the ways of everything equine!"

Jodie met him halfway. "If you think Luke can be indoctrinated into anything he isn't interested in then you don't know him very well. He is considering visiting Bucky's stable though."

"How did you manage that?"

She laughed as she slid down from the Buckmaster's back and folded herself into Marcus' arms. "By telling him about the house martins that live in the roof, and the robin who lives inside it."

He pulled her close, answering laughter rumbling in his chest. "Okay! I accept you seem to know how to deal with my son far better than I do but don't expect too much Jodie. Meeting Bucky in his own garden is one thing, sitting on a horse in a strange place and surrounded by other people is entirely another."

"I know," she accepted his kiss with enthusiasm. "Now are you going to come and see what I've achieved so far or not?"

* * *

Luke was still drawing when they walked around the house to where he was sitting. He slanted a glance towards them, looked back at his drawing and then started to put his pencils away. Jodie smiled at him.

142

"Your dad wants to say hello to Bucky today too. Is that okay Luke?"

He nodded as he snapped his pencil box shut. Then he stood up and handed Jodie the sketch he'd been drawing. She looked at it for a long time before she replied. When she did there was a slight catch in her voice.

"Thank you Luke. It's a lovely picture. I'm going to pin it on my office wall so everyone who visits me can admire it."

"No! No! No! It's just for Jodie." He shook his head fast, his voice rising in pitch with every word.

She waited until she was sure he was listening before she answered him. "I know it's just for me Luke. Thank you. I'm not going to give it to anyone else; I just want other people to be able to see it as well because it's so beautiful. May I do that? May I show it to other people as long as I don't let them touch it?"

He pondered her suggestion for several minutes while Marcus watched in fascination. Eventually, after double-checking she definitely wouldn't let anyone else touch the picture, he nodded.

She smiled her satisfaction as she returned it to the table and secured it with Luke's pencil box to stop it blowing away. Then she held out her hand. "Come and see Bucky now. It's past six o'clock so he'll be waiting for you."

To Marcus' complete amazement Luke reached out and grasped Jodie's fingers. "How did you do that?" he whispered. "Normally he won't let anyone touch him."

Jodie ignored him, as did Luke. Slightly put out to find himself relegated to the sidelines, he followed them to where Jodie had tied Buckmaster to a tree. The horse gave a soft whicker of greeting as they approached.

Luke made a very similar sound deep in his throat. Then he laughed. Jodie smiled at him. "Are you going to pat Bucky now?"

Immediately he backed away although he still kept hold of her fingers. Completely unfazed, Jodie rooted around in her pocket with her other hand and produced a carrot.

"Okay. You can do it later."

She held out the carrot as she spoke and Bucky seized it from her hand with his usual delicacy. As he munched it Luke shifted from one foot to the other making more noises, each one uncannily like Bucky's welcoming whicker. Jodie smiled at him.

"Are you talking to Bucky?"

He nodded and then pointed to her pocket. She pretended ignorance. "What do you want?"

"Bucky needs another carrot."

"Give it to him then?" Jodie pulled a second carrot from her pocket and offered it to him. For a moment Marcus thought he was going to refuse but then he reached out with his free hand and took it from her. Then, pulling his fingers from hers he placed the carrot on his flat palm with the precision Jodie had used, before moving closer to Buckmaster.

The big horse waited quietly. He didn't make any attempt to take the carrot. It was almost as if he could sense Luke's trepidation and was determined not to frighten him.

Jodie kept her voice low as she encouraged Luke to move even closer. "He won't hurt you. See how he's just waiting for you to give him the carrot. He knows it's rude to snatch."

Finally, Luke's hand was underneath Buckmaster's nose. Jodie held it steady as she murmured softly. Immediately the horse dipped his head and took the carrot. His whiskers tickled Luke's hand, startling him for just a moment. Then he laughed and it was a normal, joyful, boy's laugh. Jodie smiled.

"Well done. See how Bucky's nodding at you. When he nods he's saying thank you."

Luke stared up at the big chestnut for a moment then he put out his hand again and touched his flank very gently. Buckmaster swung his head around to look at him and as he did so he made a soft whickering noise again. Luke laughed and then he patted him several times as he made answering sounds in his own throat.

Jodie pretended not to see the tears gathering in Marcus's eyes as she encouraged Luke to explore the short hair on Buckmaster's shoulders with his fingers. Then she guided his hand upwards to his thick mane and let him explore the different texture. Finally, she persuaded him to pat the horse's nose, and when he felt the velvety softness of the skin around Buckmaster's nostrils Luke gave an exclamation of delight and rubbed his face against it.

Gently Jodie disengaged him. "I think Bucky is tired now Luke. He needs to go home and go to bed. He'll come and see you again tomorrow though. Please ask Mrs. Cotton for some carrots because I haven't got any more at home."

Luke grinned at her. "Mrs. Cotton has lots of carrots. I eat carrots too."

"I know you do but I'm sure she'll have enough for Bucky."

She vaulted up into Buckmaster's saddle as she spoke. Then she looked at Marcus. "Is it okay if I leave Luke with you? Normally I would take him indoors and hand him over to Mrs. Cotton."

He gave her a wry smile. "I guess I deserve that. Sorry for not believing in you."

She grinned down to where he was standing with Luke. "You're forgiven. I didn't always believe in you if you remember."

"So you didn't. You learned though."

"Mmm. So I did."

Their eyes met. Although the sun had dipped behind the trees, it was still bright enough for Jodie to see his expression, and what she saw made her breath catch in her throat. If that was how much he wanted her then it was time she did something about it.

"You could always marry me." He reached up and caught hold of her hand, able to read her thoughts despite the deepening gloom.

She shook her head. "You know I can't Marcus...but we'll find a way and soon. I promise."

145

# Chapter Twenty-three

Izzie was sitting at the kitchen table when Jodie eventually made it back to the cottage in the stable yard. She shook her head as her sister sank down into a chair opposite her and pulled off her boots.

"You and Marcus work too hard. Does he know about your daily visits with Luke yet?"

"He does now."

"Good or not good?"

"A bit of both. It took a while to convince him but he's more or less onside."

"Well that's something I suppose. I hope you like pasta bake…even though it doesn't look like the picture in the recipe book," Izzie dismissed all thoughts of Marcus as she got up and peered into the oven.

Jodie stared at her in amazement. "You actually cooked something?"

"Yep. I decided it was time I helped out a bit more."

"Don't be silly. You already do more than enough. You help with the horses and the riding program. You do your share of the cleaning and tidying. You even produce meals from time to time."

"Yes. Cold ones. Cold cuts with chutney, and other exotic things like cheese sandwiches. Not real meals. Besides I need to learn to cook so I can look after myself when I leave home."

Jodie flinched at her words. Although she knew Izzie was going, and probably sooner rather than later, it was still something she didn't want to think about until it actually happened. She didn't want to think about it until she was

146

sure her sister was able to sleep alone at night either.

Izzie gave a wry smile. "Don't look like that. I need you to believe in me."

Pushing herself up from the chair Jodie reached out and hugged her. "It's not about belief, it's about fright...my fright. I don't want to let you go and yet I know I must."

Izzie hugged her back, hard. "Yeah...well you'll soon get over it. The minute I'm gone Marcus will be here every night, unless you move in with him."

Jodie shook her head. "That's not going to happen because I'm not going to leave the cottage."

"Why not? Letting somebody else move in here wouldn't stop you being manager, and if you decided to give up altogether Carol would jump at the chance to take over from you."

"I know, but I just can't. Don't ask me to explain. It's too complicated."

"No it's not. Not if you really love Marcus, and you do, don't you?"

Instead of answering, Jodie changed the subject. "I'm going to have a shower now, assuming the pasta bake will wait."

* * *

Jodie mulled over Izzie's words as the hot water sluiced over her. If only it were that simple, but if she moved in with Marcus she would have to give up the cottage, and with it the one thing she had fought so long and hard for, her independence. That she would also be branded as his mistress and almost certainly considered a money-grabber was another factor, though a less important one. She could weather that even if she made the papers, but she knew she would find it more difficult to cope with Mrs. Cotton's disapproval and that of the rest of Luke's care team. She also knew it wasn't possible to live with someone as famous and as wealthy as Marcus without the rest of the world waiting for the relationship to fail, and now his new studio was often full of musicians there would be even more people judging her.

She could always marry him of course. He had made it very clear that marriage was what he wanted, and from the outside it seemed the obvious solution, except it wasn't. Deep down her distrust of marriage and long term relationships simmered and brewed. She had seen too much heartbreak to want to throw all her dice on the one square that was Marcus Lewis. Even though she loved him with a passion that was all consuming she was sure it wouldn't last. It never did. Somewhere, sometime, he was going to let her down because that's what men did. The thought brought her back to her present dilemma. Izzie. How was she going to keep her promise to find time alone with Marcus while her sister was still living at home?

* * *

Izzie solved it for her when she returned to the kitchen by announcing she was going to the studio as soon as they had finished eating.

"I've a session with a voice coach," she said as she dished up the pasta. "Marcus says I need to learn how to protect my throat more before I start singing in public."

"How long is the session?" Jodie tried hard to keep her voice neutral.

Izzie read her mind. "Long enough."

* * *

When Jodie answered the knock on the door she was wearing a flimsy negligee that had once belonged to her mother and her raven's wing hair was hanging down her back in a silken curtain. With a swift intake of breath Marcus picked her up and carried her upstairs without a word. By the time he found the right bedroom and lowered her onto the bed they were both trembling. Lying down beside her he began to kiss her, gently at first but then with a passion that made them both forget where they were as their whole world slowly spiraled into an all-consuming

148

need.

Much later, lying in a tangle of arms and legs, their faces only inches apart on the pillow, they smiled at one another.

"Your sister has the best ideas," Marcus whispered as he twirled his finger through a strand of Jodie's hair.

Immediately she stiffened in his arms. "This has nothing to do with Izzie except she happens to be out for once."

He gathered her closer, so their lips were almost touching. "Ah don't Jodie. Of course it has something to do with her, why else would I be able to stay right here all night."

Twisting herself out of his arms she sat up and glared down at him. "What do you mean, stay here all night? That is so not going to happen Marcus, not with Izzie in the next room."

He stared up at her. "You mean you don't know she is staying over at my house tonight?"

"Why would I when she hasn't told me anything about it?"

He laughed then and it was a genuine burst of amusement. "She is going to be wasted on the stage you know. She could be a master criminal and rule the world if she wanted to, because she's totally without shame."

"What exactly did she tell you?" Jodie didn't join in with his laughter. Instead she resisted as he tried to pull her close again.

He sighed. "She said her therapist thought it was time she tried to sleep away from home on her own. Apparently he said it ought to be somewhere familiar, and suggested my house."

"And you believed her?"

"Why wouldn't I? Besides she had already spoken to Mrs. Cotton about it by the time she told me. She told her all about her sleep problems too, and apparently Mrs Cotton is perfectly happy for her to use my house as a testing ground. She said they had chosen tonight because Izzie had told her I wasn't going to be there, so you see I

149

have nowhere else to go unless you want to blow your sister's cover."

"I can't believe she's so devious," Jodie ignored his attempt at humor.

"What Izzie? Come on Jodie, being devious is her signature behavior. Besides, you have to admit it's a good idea," he maneuvered himself into a sitting position and tried to pull her back against his chest.

She resisted, still frowning, and then reached for her cell phone. "But what if she isn't alright? What if she has one of her nightmares? I'm not going to let her do it. If she wakes up screaming in a strange house in the middle of the night she could put herself back years. She should have tested it out here first."

Marcus closed his hand around hers so she couldn't tap in the numbers to her sister's cell phone. "And what if she's perfectly fine? You can't throw this back in her face, not when she's trying so hard."

"I'm not...I won't...not when it's a genuine attempt to move on, but to do it just so we can sleep together, that's not the right reason. It's not even something she should be thinking about."

"You're not her mother Jodie, even though you act as if you are, and if you think she doesn't have a view on sex then you need to come to the studio and watch her flirting with some of the musicians. Izzie is trying to grow up...so have some faith in her and let go."

"I...does she really flirt?" Her eyes were wide as she picked up on what he had just told her.

He grinned. "And how! But you don't need to worry, she isn't going to sleep with any of them, she's just testing her powers. She's doing all the things you didn't have the time to do when you were her age. Let her enjoy them."

"How come you know so much about teenage girls?"

He shook his head. "You don't want to know."

At last she relaxed, dropping the cell phone back onto the bedside table. "You're probably right. I don't want to know if it has anything to do with the days when you used to tour. I know you're right about Izzie too, but it's just so

150

difficult...I can't believe how craftily she's maneuvered us into this, how easily I fell for it."

"Well you did, so how about we make the most of it?" Marcus started to stroke her shoulders and then changed his mind and let his hand dip lower until it brushed against her breasts. With a shudder she turned towards him, her eyes suddenly dark with a building desire that blotted out everything except wanting him. His smile was triumphant as he lifted her on top of him and before long, hidden beneath the glossy curtain of her hair, they forgot all about Izzie and concentrated, instead, on the whisper of skin on skin and the salty taste of their love.

# Chapter Twenty-four

When Jodie woke Marcus was propped up on one elbow watching her. He leaned over and kissed her. "Hello."

"Hello," her voice was full of sleep, her eyes soft with memory as she twined her arms around his neck and pulled him closer. With a groan he gathered her to him.

"I wasn't going to do this. I was going to creep out before people start turning up to feed the horses."

She pulled back a little and smiled. "To protect my reputation?"

"Something like that."

"Well you don't need to worry because you can sneak out the back way."

Supporting his weight on his elbows he looked down at her. "I don't want to sneak Jodie. I want everyone to know how I feel about you. I want everyone to know how much…"

"Sshh!" she put her fingers on his lips and then followed them with her mouth, tracing their outline with her tongue. It was all it took for him to lose himself in her arms and it was a long, long time before they spoke again. When they did it was because the rattling of the gate disturbed them.

Panic stricken she leapt from the bed and made for the door. Marcus chuckled at the expression on her face. "Much as I appreciate the view I think you'd better put some clothes on before you go outside."

Hastily she pulled on a pair of jeans. Then she seized a sweater and headed for the stairs. By the time she returned Marcus was fully dressed and sitting on the side of the bed. He grinned at her. "How did you get out of that?"

152

"I told them the truth…that I overslept."

"And they bought it?"

"They're a bit worried I'm sickening for something because it's the first time the gate has ever been locked. I'm usually up hours before they arrive."

"Mmm…well perhaps it's time you changed your habits. Marry me Jodie, or if you still can't do that, then just come and live with me and let someone else do the early morning stuff. You've done it for long enough."

Without answering she stripped off her clothes and then rummaged through her wardrobe for clean underwear, a fresh polo shirt and a pair of jodhpurs. Marcus waited, enjoying her lack of inhibition but frustrated by her silence. She didn't speak until she had brushed the tangles from her hair and pleated it into a tidy plait. Then she turned and looked at him with eyes full of regret.

"I can't marry you Marcus, and I won't live with you either, so if this isn't enough you need to tell me now."

He reached her in two strides and locked her in his arms. "I'll take you any way I can but I'm not going to give up. You'll marry me one day."

She shook her head, smiling through a sudden blur of tears. "Go away. The sneak exit is via the kitchen but you can have coffee before you go."

"Not if it's the stuff you usually serve," he dipped his head and kissed her, then followed her down the stairs.

Laughing she pushed him out the back door, wriggling away from him as he attempted to kiss her again. "Wait until this evening."

He caught hold of her wrist. "Is that a promise?"

"That depends on Izzie." As she spoke she suddenly remembered why Marcus was standing in her kitchen. He saw the panic wash across her face.

"I'll check on her as soon as I get home."

She nodded; relieved she didn't have to explain anything. Then she turned away and left him. Marcus watched her go, his heart full. He had never doubted his feelings for her but now, after spending a night in her arms, he knew he couldn't live without her.

153

# Chapter Twenty-five

"Jodie you've got to come!" Izzie's voice was a screech down the telephone but underneath it Jodie could hear the wobble of tears.

With her heart in the pit of her stomach, she tried for calm. "Hang on. I'll be there as soon as I can…just take some deep breaths and…"

She stared at the cell phone. Izzie had cut the call. With her imagination in overdrive she abandoned the paperwork she'd been checking and rushed out into the yard. Carol was talking to one of the young volunteers who helped muck out the stables at the weekend. She barged into their conversation.

"Carol I've got to go. There's a problem with Izzie. Will you hold the fort 'til I get back?"

Without waiting for an answer she jumped into the Land Rover and crashed it into gear, all the while wondering why Marcus hadn't called her.

* * *

She found out within moments of buzzing for the gates to open because when they swung inwards so she could drive up to the house, the first thing she saw was Izzie running towards her. With no thought that she was blocking the driveway, she cut the engine and jumped out, ready to defuse whatever nightmare had toppled her sister into hysteria.

"I knew it was a bad idea for you to sleep over," she said, bracing herself. Izzie shook her head impatiently, grabbing Jodie's hand and pulling her towards the house as she spoke.

"It's not me. It's Marcus who needs you, and Luke."

* * *

Blue was lying in his basket and the kitchen was full of the sound of his labored breathing. When he saw Jodie he tried to wag his tail. Marcus was sitting on the floor next to him, his face pinched with grief.

"I knew it was going to happen soon," he said, without looking at her. "I just didn't want it to be yet."

She crouched down next to him and reached out and caressed the old dog's silky ears. Close to she could see the rapid involuntary movement of his cloudy eyes. It was something she had seen years before when a horse had collapsed in front of her.

"He's suffering from nystagmus Marcus. I think he's had a stroke."

He nodded. "That's what the vet said when I called him. He says he'll come as soon as he can."

Fighting her need to put her arms around him and hold him close, she stood up. "What about Luke? Does he know what's happening?"

"I don't know. Izzie's been looking after him because there's no one else here. Mrs. Cotton left for a doctor's appointment as soon as I got home, and nobody else is due yet."

* * *

She found them in the garden. All the bird feeders were lined up on the patio table and Izzie was helping Luke to fill them with nuts and seeds. She looked up when Jodie walked towards them, her eyes full of questions. Jodie shook her head as she pulled out a chair and sat down. Luke ignored her until he'd finished what he was doing then he spoke to her as if she had been sitting next to him all along.

"I need some more birdseed and some nuts, and a bird table."

155

"You'd better make a list," Jodie told him. Then she and Izzie helped him to hang the feeders on the various branches he had chosen when she first gave them to him. It took quite a while because each one had a special place and he was very picky about it. Finally, they finished.

"Now it's clearing up time," Jodie said. He stared at her.

"Mrs. Cotton clears up."

"Mrs. Cotton is not here right now. She's gone out, so you'll have to do it Luke."

He shook his head. "Mrs. Cotton always clears up."

She sighed, wondering anew how Marcus could have allowed him to reach the age of eleven with no sense of responsibility at all. She had worked with children for far too long to accept his disability as an excuse. Luke was bright and he liked to learn, so if she could teach less able children to care for the horses they rode, then she was sure Luke could learn to clear up after himself. Immediately she castigated herself for having such uncharitable thoughts while Marcus was sitting with his dying dog. Now was not the time to push Luke either. He was going to have a hard enough time coping with Blue's death. She knew he and the old dog were exactly the same age, so now, as well as having to get used to a new home, he was going to have to cope with losing one of the lynchpins of his life. She wondered if anyone had ever talked to him about Blue and told him that because he was very old, he was going to die.

Taking a deep breath, she smiled at him. "Well we'll leave it for Mrs. Cotton this time then. Let's go indoors now?"

He followed her into the kitchen where Marcus was still sitting beside Blue, gently rubbing the old dog's head. He frowned when he saw Luke.

"He shouldn't be here. It will just upset him."

"So will discovering Blue has gone but without knowing why."

He glared at her. "I don't want him here when the vet comes."

"He won't be, but he has to understand what's

156

happening, even if it causes problems. Blue has been part of his life ever since he was born so you can't let him just disappear with no explanation."

"Where is Blue going?" Luke's question sliced through their conversation as he walked across to where the old dog was lying. His eyes were closed now but when he heard Luke's voice they slatted open. For a long moment the boy and the dog looked at one another. Then Blue gave an enormous sigh and stopped breathing.

* * *

Much later, after Marcus had vented the worst of his grief by digging a deep hole at the end of the garden and laying Blue's body in it, he sat at the kitchen counter with his head resting on one hand. Jodie pushed a mug towards him.

"Drink your coffee while I check on Luke."

He didn't answer but when she moved past him he put out his free hand and pulled her to him. With a sob she wrapped her arms around him and they clung together for a long moment. Then she gently but firmly extricated herself, knowing Izzie and Luke needed her more.

They were sitting together watching a wildlife DVD. Izzie's eyes were red but Luke was too intent on what was happening on the screen to notice when Jodie joined them. Sitting beside Izzie she raised a questioning eyebrow.

"He doesn't seem to care," Izzie whispered. "He hasn't said anything at all about Blue even though he knows he's dead. All he's worried about is whether Mrs. Cotton will be back in time to cook his lunch."

Jodie shook her head. "Because he doesn't experience things the same as other people he might never grieve for him, or it might happen next week, next month, or even next year, and that's something Marcus is going to find really hard to deal with."

* * *

157

It proved to be harder than she had anticipated because once Luke accepted Blue was dead he spent all his time talking about him, and about what had happened to him when he died. Within a few days an obsession with death had replaced his interest in birds and he spent all his time drawing and labeling animal skeletons. Unable to cope with it, and with his incessant questions, Marcus retreated into his studio, only reappearing at the end of each day a few minutes before Luke's bedtime.

Izzie spent a lot of time in the studio as well, preparing for her first public performance. She came home each night though and to Jodie's dismay she began to leave her bedroom door wide open again. She lost weight too, and there were permanent shadows beneath her eyes.

At her wit's end, Jodie divided her time between her work at the riding school and Luke, Marcus and Izzie, in the forlorn hope things would soon revert to something more manageable.

She visited Luke at the end of every day while Marcus was still in the studio. She looked at his drawings and answered his incessant questions, she talked to Mrs. Cotton about how best to distract him, and she tried to persuade him to say hello to Buckmaster again. He wouldn't though, even though he knew the big chestnut horse was waiting patiently outside. He wouldn't even talk about him. Every time Jodie mentioned his name he clapped his hands over his ears and started making an irritating clicking noise with his tongue.

Finally, she had had enough, and instead of waiting for Marcus to leave the studio and come up to the house to see her, like he did every evening, she went to find him instead. The sound that washed over her as she pushed open the door made the hairs on the back of her neck stand up. She had never heard music like it. Every note was a cry of pain, every phrase the memory of a broken heart. Silently she slipped into the studio and sat on the floor just inside the door. By the time Marcus saw her, her cheeks were wet with tears; tears for him, for Luke, for Blue, for Izzie, and for her own lost dreams. With an exclamation of disgust, he

158

banged down the lid of the piano and hurried across to where she was crouching against the wall. Gathering her in his arms he rocked her to and fro.

"Please don't cry Jodie. I know I've been impossible and I'm sorry. I know I should be better at dealing with Luke but he makes me so angry that the only way I can stop myself from shaking him is to stay in the studio."

Burying her face in his shoulder she shook her head. "I wasn't crying about you…I…it was that piece you were playing… it turned me inside out. My nerve endings are all on the outside now, along with every painful memory and every tear I've ever shed."

He brushed her hair with his lips. "It's the only way I know to make sense of things. Instead of thinking about other people and about how they feel, all I want to do is shut myself in the studio and turn my own feelings into music."

Tilting her head back she gave him a watery smile. "Anyone listening to the piece you've just played will know you feel exactly like they do and they'll forgive you."

Without answering he kissed her, licking at the salt of her tears with his tongue before probing lower to where her mouth was waiting. Within moments they had forgotten everything but their need for one another and when Marcus swept her up into his arms and carried her across to the huge couch that took up half of one wall, Jodie clung to him as if she were drowning.

He untangled her arms with a groan. "Let me lock the door."

By the time he turned back to where she was sitting she had shed her fleece and polo shirt and was tugging at her jodhpurs.

* * *

Later, sprawled across his chest, Jodie looked at Marcus. The strain had gone from his face but he still looked tired and miserable. She ran her fingertips across the bow of his lips and then smiled as a shudder went through him. He saw her expression and grinned at her.

"Witch."

"I wish," she rolled away from him. "If I were a witch I would be able to put everything right with a magic potion."

"You do that already for me. You enchanted me when I first met you and I'm still under your spell."

"That's not what I meant and you know it. Stop flirting with me and be serious."

He turned his head to look at her, reveling in the purity of her profile and the tangle of her hair even as he answered. "I'm not flirting. I mean it Jodie. And if you want to be serious, how about agreeing to marry me now you know everything about me, warts and all?"

She sighed. "Not that sort of serious…the how do we help Luke and Izzie sort of serious."

He frowned and then propped himself up on the couch and wedged a cushion under his head. "What's wrong with Izzie? I thought the therapy was working."

Squirming around to face him, she shrugged. "It was but now it's not. She hasn't been the same ever since Blue died."

"Nor have any of us, but surely it doesn't mean her old problems have come back."

"It does when she starts to leave her bedroom door wide open again every night, and when she barely raises a smile even when she's talking about music. And she's hardly been to see Luke at all."

"Well you can't blame her for that, not if she's feeling down. Who wants to spend all their time talking about death and dying, and what happens to bodies when they're dead?"

"Luke does, and that's what I mean about being serious Marcus. He needs to work this out of his system before it becomes a total obsession, but he can't do it without you."

"Me? You and Izzie get far more out of him in five minutes than I do in a day. No, I'm not the person you need for this."

160

Wriggling around even further, she faced him. "That's where you're wrong. Luke is behaving like he is because of you. He doesn't understand grief. Although he knows Blue has died it doesn't mean he understands why everyone is sad. He just knows it has something to do with dying and he's trying to make sense of it."

"And you're such an expert because...?"

"Because I took the trouble to ask an expert about it," Jodie's face was full of sudden fury as she answered him.

"An expert who knows more than Mrs. Cotton or the other people who care for him every day?"

"Yes! A real expert Marcus. Someone who is trained to help children with autism who are grieving, and who understands what Luke is going through. Mrs. Cotton is a lovely lady but she's not enough for him. Nor are the teams of people who keep him tethered to his routine. You've spent a fortune bringing most of them up here with you just to keep him happy when what he actually needs are challenges, lots of challenges. He also needs his father to help him cope with them, whereas at the moment all he's got is someone who doesn't want him around at all."

"Well I'm sorry to be such a disappointment but I've been there and tried that, and it didn't work." Marcus swung his legs off the couch and reached for his jeans. Then he started to laugh.

Jodie scowled at him. "What's so funny?"

"You are...we are...discussing this while we're both stark naked. This is not exactly pillow talk is it?"

It only took a moment for Jodie's scowl to slip and then disappear and soon she was sitting on his lap, her arms twined around his neck, her lips whispering across his cheek. "I'm sorry. You're right, this isn't the time, but we do have to talk about it Marcus. Luke needs help. Izzie needs help. We all do."

He tightened his arms around her. "Okay, you win. I promise to talk about it...but...not...right...now." He punctuated each word with a kiss and soon Izzie and Luke had been forgotten again.

# Chapter Twenty-six

Marcus was as good as his word. The next day he was waiting for Jodie, and when she went in search of Luke he followed her, and then mirrored her behavior. He admired the pictures of the skeletons that were threatening to overwhelm his son's sitting room, and then listened to his non-stop commentary about death. Finally, when Luke paused for breath, he spoke to him.

"Do you remember what happened when Blue died Luke?"

"You buried him."

"Yes. I buried him in the garden. Do you know why I did that?"

"So he won't go away."

"No. He's dead Luke. He can't go anywhere. I buried him in the garden so I can remember him. I can sit by his grave and think about him whenever I want to."

"And what happens when a dead body is buried Luke?" Jodie interrupted because she knewA Marcus was being too fanciful for a child who only dealt in facts.

To Marcus's distress, his son immediately went into graphic detail about decomposition, but when he started to protest Jodie grabbed his hand and squeezed it hard. With enormous difficulty he took his cue from her and swallowed his words as he waited for Luke to finish. Eventually Jodie slipped a question into the tiny pauses between his son's words.

"And what else happens when a body decomposes Luke?"

He stared at her. "It feeds the worms and the insects."

Ignoring the pained expression on Marcus' face, she nodded. "And that makes them fat and healthy, just the way the birds like them. Is that what Blue's body is doing Luke?"

His eyes opened wide as comprehension dawned. Then he turned to Marcus with a beaming smile. "Blue is feeding the birds."

\* \* \*

"That was very painful," Marcus walked her out to where Buckmaster was waiting.

Jodie twined her fingers with his. "I know, and you'll probably have to go through it all again tomorrow, but it's a start. It'll get easier I promise."

"I guess I need to spend some time with your expert."

She squeezed his hand. "Will you...if I organize it?"

"Mmm...but I want you to do something for me in return."

He saw the question in her eyes as he bent to kiss her. "I want you to think harder about marrying me Jodie. This living apart and have to snatch at moments alone together is ridiculous. I want you in my house and in my bed and I really don't understand why you don't feel the same, not when you've proved in every other way exactly how you feel about me."

\* \* \*

"What am I going to do Bucky?" Jodie put her hand under Buckmaster's soft muzzle and smiled as he blew into it. "I want to live with him but how can I do that when it might all go pear-shaped tomorrow? What if he meets someone else while he's off on one of his trips to California; someone who understands all about music; someone who would fit his lifestyle better than I ever will?"

Buckmaster regarded her patiently with his liquid brown eyes. He liked the sound of her voice even though he didn't understand the words. He knew, too, when she was sad. And she was sad now, which was why he hadn't started to eat even though he wanted to.

Jodie laughed at him as she secured the straps on his blanket. "Alright, I'm going greedy boy. Sleep tight."

He snorted as she pulled the stable door shut behind her and she was still laughing when she walked into the kitchen. She stopped smiling as soon as she saw Izzie though because her sister was sitting in front of the computer staring at an image that almost filled the screen. It was a picture of their mother. She half turned when she heard Jodie.

"Why didn't you tell me?"

"Tell you what?"

"That we once had a sister. Why didn't you tell me about how she was delivered at the side of the road after Mamma died?"

Ignoring her question Jodie peered at the screen. Her heart sank when she saw the old newspaper article she was reading.

"How did you find that?"

"I used a search engine. How else? Did you think you could keep this from me forever? Didn't you think I had a right to know?"

"No…yes…of course I did, but not yet. I didn't want to tell you until you were old enough to understand, until…"

"…until I'd stopped having nightmares. Until I'd been cured by the therapist you and Marcus thought I needed."

"Do need," Jodie corrected her. "If you want to leave home and cope on your own then you do need help Izzie."

"No I don't…not now I know the truth. Not now I know I wasn't imagining things when I peered out the window of the car. I really did see a man doing something to Mama didn't I, but I was far too young to understand what it was? When he got up and walked towards me carrying a baby covered in blood it was because he's just performed an emergency caesarian right there on the roadside, not because he'd killed Mama. She was already

164

dead from the accident wasn't she? But I was so scared by what I saw that my mind turned him into a monster, and I slid down onto the floor and pulled the blanket that had been covering me right over my head because I thought he was coming to get me…and I've never been able to stop thinking that, not until now. Every time I woke up screaming at night it was because I was sure he was there in the bedroom with me, and I knew if he ever found me alone he would kill me too.

"I'll be okay now I understand though. What I saw was true wasn't it? I didn't imagine it. There was a man and there was a lot of blood, but he wasn't a monster, he was a doctor who was trying to help?"

Horrified, Jodie just stared at her. How had this happened? How had she got it so wrong? Why didn't she know about her sister's monster? Why had she just accepted it when the child psychologists told her Izzie was suffering from Post Traumatic Stress Disorder and that when she had nightmares she was reliving the car crash? Nobody had ever mentioned a monster, not even Izzie herself.

"I didn't know," she whispered, sinking into the chair opposite. "I thought…everyone thought you were just frightened by the memory of the crash. How come you never told anyone?"

Izzie shook her head. "I tried to once, but the woman I told said I was imagining things. She said I'd been so frightened by the crash my brain was making things up. She told me there were no such things as monsters."

"But why didn't you tell me?" Jodie couldn't hide the hurt in her voice as she remembered all the nights she had held her sister close while she waited for her terrified sobs to subside.

After a long pause Izzie's face crumpled, and suddenly she was the little girl in Jodie's arms again. "Because I didn't want you to be frightened of him as well," she sobbed.

* * *

165

Jodie was still wide awake when her cell phone rang. She had been staring into the darkness for what seemed like hours, her eyes gritty and sore from all the tears she and Izzie had shared that evening. Marcus heard them in her voice as soon as she spoke.

"I'm fine," she told him. "Really I am Marcus…it's just this evening has been…difficult."

He listened as she recounted the long conversation she had had with Izzie over a scratch meal of bread and cheese, not interrupting even when she told him how Blue's death had triggered her sister's memories.

"When she stood in your garden and watched you lower Blue's body into the grave, for some unaccountable reason she had a flash back. I don't understand why it happened and I don't think she does either, but suddenly she had a clear memory of our mother lying dead at the roadside. She had repressed it for years, only remembering the monster and the blood in her nightmares."

"So that's why she decided to go searching for her on the Internet?" Marcus prompted when she paused.

"Yes. And it didn't take her long to find the newspaper reports or the court proceedings that followed. I should have realized she would do something like that eventually and told her everything a long time ago, then she wouldn't have spent years thinking she was imagining things. I haven't been helping her Marcus. By trying to protect her I've just been making things worse."

"Rubbish! And I bet Izzie doesn't think so either. She doesn't, does she?"

"No…but I do Marcus… and it hurts to know how badly I've let her down."

\* \* \*

Jodie woke as the first fingers of dawn clawed at the horizon and after a few minutes of tossing and turning she gave up, threw back her covers and began to pull on her clothes.

166

Buckmaster gave a soft whinny of pleasure when she unlatched the door to his stable, and before long she had saddled him and led him out of the yard. Once outside she vaulted up onto his back and turned his nose in the direction of the beach. The dark figure that loomed up when she approached the bridleway sent a momentary quiver of fear through her until she realized it was Marcus.

"What are you doing here?" she asked him.

"Waiting for you."

They stared at one another, their eyes shadowed by the early morning gloom, and then she was out of the saddle and in his arms.

"I've made such a mess of everything," she whispered, pressing her cheek against his jacket. "If it wasn't for me, Izzie would have been over her trauma years ago."

"You don't know any such thing and you'll never know it anymore than I'll ever know whether Lucia meant to kill herself. Sometimes we just have to accept things and move on. It took me a long time and a lot of therapy to learn it's the only way."

"But what if I can't move on? What if I remember it every time I look at her?"

"Then you'll have to find something else to think about, which brings me to my next idea. How about if I bring Luke to see you and Bucky later on today."

She knew it wasn't something he wanted to do; knew he was only suggesting it to take her mind off Izzie, and she loved him for it even while she reluctantly shook her head.

"He's not ready Marcus. You can't just bring him because you feel like it. He's got to want to come himself. He's got to ask to see Bucky instead of putting his hands over his ears every time I mention his name, and making that stupid clicking noise that drives everyone mad."

"Well bring him for breakfast then. Tether him close to the dining room. Maybe Luke will change his mind if he sees him outside the window."

She shook her head again. "I can't. I need to get back before Izzie wakes up. Today of all days she needs me to be there for her."

He led her back to Buckmaster and boosted her back into the saddle. "You're always there for her. Stop saying no and leave Izzie to me. It's pancakes all round at eight o'clock."

* * *

She heard their laughter as she approached the kitchen and was surprised at the effect it had on her. She hadn't known how uptight she was until the knot in her throat loosened and a curl of warmth flushed her cheeks.

"I've just demoted Izzie to commis chef because she's rubbish at tossing pancakes," Marcus told her as she pushed open the door.

"That's so not fair. I only missed the pan because he spoke to me at the vital moment!" Izzie grinned at Jodie as she looked up from where she was busy clearing up splashes of pancake mix from the kitchen counter.

Noting with relief that color had returned to her sister's cheeks and the haunted expression of the past few days had faded from her face, Jodie forced herself to join in with the banter, and then to applaud Marcus' expertise as he ladled batter into the hot pan and tossed a perfect golden pancake.

"I guess you'd better find some plates and cutlery," he said as the pile began to grow.

"What about Luke? Surely he like pancakes too?" Izzie was searching through the kitchen drawers as she spoke so she missed the irritation that flickered across Marcus' face. Jodie didn't though.

"I'll go find him," she said.

* * *

Luke was halfway through his breakfast. His eyes were wide as he stared at Jodie across the top of his glass of orange juice. She knew seeing her at an unfamiliar time of day might be difficult for him but she was determined to try. Mrs. Cotton was sitting at the table too, and after a moment's thought Jodie directed her remarks to her.

"Marcus is making pancakes."

Realizing what she wanted, Mrs. Cotton responded with a smile. "Luke likes pancakes. He always pours maple syrup over them."

Luke put down his glass and returned to his scrambled eggs without any indication he'd heard them, but Jodie picked up the cue.

"Do you know where the maple syrup is Mrs. Cotton?"

The older woman shook her head. "No I don't. Luke might remember where it's kept though."

Jodie turned to him. "Do you know where it is Luke?"

Although he gave her a slanting look he didn't answer. Instead he carried on eating his scrambled egg and toast with slow deliberation. With a sigh Jodie made for the door.

"I'll see if I can find it myself before my pancake get cold."

As she made her way back to the kitchen her heart bled for the little boy she had left hunched over his breakfast tray. What had happened to the child who, when she first met him, had talked non-stop about the birds in the trees outside his balcony, and then later about the ones in his new garden? Blue's death might have sent him into a personal reality that nobody could penetrate but something else was keeping him there. She wished she knew what it was because then she might be able to find a way to help him out of the dark place he now inhabited, and if she could do that then it might help Marcus too.

She tried to remember everything she had learned about children with autism. What was she missing? Suddenly she knew the answer. Luke wouldn't be himself again until Marcus was. As long as Marcus grieved for Blue, as long as he shut himself away in his studio and poured all his feelings into his music, his son would continue to search for answers. His obsession with death was his attempt to try to understand Marcus' behavior; it wasn't about Blue at all. He was used to his father being away a lot, and to being distracted and busy when he was

169

around, but he was bright enough to know the difference between a necessary and busy absence and an absence of spirit. He didn't understand why Marcus was unhappy but he knew he was different from the person he had been before Blue died, and it frightened him.

Come to think of it, she hadn't seen him smile once since that awful morning when they had buried the old dog. Now, on her daily visits, he mostly refused to talk at all. He had stopped laughing too. That musical whoop of joy that had so often accompanied his helter-skelter rush across the terrace to see Buckmaster had disappeared completely, and it was all because of Marcus' self-absorption. She felt a surge of anger as she walked into the kitchen. He wasn't the only person on the planet who had a son with problems, so the sooner he came to terms with it and put Luke first, the better.

Izzie wiped traces of pancake from her mouth as she met Jodie's gaze. "No luck?"

She shook her head, not trusting herself to speak, and when Marcus handed her a plate with a freshly tossed pancake in the middle of it, she barely managed the trace of a smile. He frowned. Luke had obviously done something to upset her. If only she would leave him to Mrs. Cotton and her team, then she'd stop being disappointed every time he failed to respond.

"Your turn now," he said, handing the spatula to Izzie. Then he sat down opposite Jodie and watched as she began to eat. She forced herself to look at him.

"Luke was eating his breakfast."

"Mmm. He always does at eight o'clock."

"I told him you were making pancakes."

"And he ignored you...."

He stopped mid-sentence as Luke walked through the door. Without looking at any of them he made a beeline for the walk-in larder and reached for the maple syrup on the top shelf. He wasn't quite tall enough but when he looked around expectantly Jodie just pushed a chair in his direction.

"Stand on that and you'll be able to get it."

170

He stared at her for a moment because he was used to other people doing everything for him but then he dragged the chair into the larder and clambered up. He wobbled precariously against the shelving for a moment before he grabbed the bottle of syrup. She studiously ignored him, her nervousness about his lack of balance kept firmly in check.

Marcus watched, torn between fear and irritation. Luke had fallen off too many things over the years for him to see him climbing onto a chair with much confidence, and he unconsciously took several steps forward, ready to catch him if he tumbled. His irritation wasn't about Luke though. It was about Jodie. It didn't matter how much he tried, nothing he did with Luke seemed to suit her. She always found him wanting. She didn't seem to understand that he couldn't relax around Luke. Instead, having his son around as much as possible seemed to be all she wanted.

He looked across to where she still sat at the kitchen counter. She was ignoring him in the same way Luke ignored him. Bitterness washed over him as he remembered how he had listened to her sobbing her heart out over the phone the previous evening, and how he had been up at the crack of dawn to be sure of catching her on her early morning ride. Then, as quickly, he was ashamed. All she was doing was trying to help him. What sort of father was he to be jealous of his own son? With an effort he smiled as Luke placed the bottle of syrup in the middle of the kitchen counter.

"Well done. Now I'm going to make you a pancake."

* * *

"It's time I wasn't here. People will be waiting for me." Jodie picked up her riding hat and crop and made for the door, but as she passed Marcus he reached out a long arm and encircled her waist.

"Hey, what about a thank you kiss?"

She wrinkled her nose at him. "Is this what's going to happen every time you cook something for me?"

He grinned at her, suddenly a lot more lighthearted because, despite his earlier irritation, breakfast had been surprisingly good. He watched Luke and Izzie giggling over her attempt to drizzle the remains of the maple syrup into a face shape on her final pancake and wondered if this was what family life would be like if he could ever persuade Jodie to marry him.

"I might ask for a bigger reward sometimes," he whispered as he lowered his mouth.

She pulled away so swiftly that his lips only grazed hers. "If you want a reward then spend the day with Luke instead of hiding in your studio. He needs you Marcus whether you like it or not, and if you actually spent some time with him you might be surprised at how much fun he can be."

His brows knitted together in a frown as she blew his good humor away. It was back to Luke again. He could count on the fingers of one hand how often they had been alone together since he had moved into the village and even then family or work responsibilities had intruded. He remembered their argument in the studio the previous day, and he remembered, too, how he had sneaked out of Jodie's cottage to protect her reputation when all he wanted was to tell the world how he felt about her.

As if she could read his mind, her expression softened. Standing on tiptoe she pressed her lips to his. "Try it," she said, and then the kitchen door slammed shut behind her.

# Chapter Twenty-seven

Jodie was too busy to give Marcus a thought for the rest of the morning. It was only when she stopped sufficiently long to grab a sandwich for lunch that she discovered the messages he'd left on her cell phone. There were three of them and they all said the same thing: Call me.

With lessons booked back-to-back until mid-afternoon, it was four o'clock before she finally managed to phone him. When she did she braced herself for his irritation.

"I'm sorry I was grumpy this morning Marcus, especially after you got up so early and then called Izzie and made pancakes for us all... I had no right to nag you about Luke either, I..."

He cut her off mid-sentence, dismissing her apology. "Is it okay if I bring him to see you at the end of the afternoon?"

"Yes, of course it is, but only if it's what he wants. I already told you that forcing him to come won't work."

She could hear the impatience in his voice. "Give me a little credit won't you. He keeps saying he wants to see Buckmaster. I don't know what put it into his head; maybe it was seeing you at breakfast. Whatever it is...he's very insistent. Izzie says it's best to let him. She says you stop teaching around four."

"She's right. I've just finished my last lesson so you can come now if you want to. Get Izzie to come home too Marcus. We haven't finished yesterday's conversation yet."

She heard him sigh. "Nor have we," he said and then he cut the call.

* * *

Jodie had been staring blindly at the accounts for five minutes when Marcus drove into the yard. Hearing the car door slam she shut down the computer and walked out to meet him, anticipating a frown or something worse. Luke might want to visit Buckmaster but from his tone of voice on the phone, it was very clear Marcus didn't. He was doing it in spite of himself rather than because he thought it might help his son. She gave an inward sigh. Why did it have to be like this when everything else in their relationship was so good?

A sudden and painful thought stopped her short as Marcus walked towards her. What if they could never resolve their differences? What if he insisted on continuing to sideline Luke? Could she live with that or would the respect she had for him slowly erode? Would she be the one to eventually walk away rather than the other way around? With a huge effort she smiled at him as they met in the middle of the yard.

"Where's Luke?"

"Izzie's taken him to see Buckmaster." Marcus didn't return her smile.

She turned away. "We'd better go join them then."

He lengthened his stride until he overtook her and then stopped and confronted her. "I thought you said she is nearly as good as you when it comes to horses and children."

"I did…she is."

"So we don't need to worry about them?"

She shook her head. "I…I guess not."

"Good, because we've got some talking to do, and before you say a word…no, it can't wait. I'm fed up with this Jodie. Fed up with wanting you in my bed every night and having to wait until you can fit me into your busy schedule. Fed up with needing to talk to you…needing to spend time with you…only to have it all taken away because something has happened to Izzie or to Luke. I'm

174

fed up with being at the bottom of your list."

She stared up at him. She was too angry to hear the raw pain in his voice. "So what do you expect me to do about it? Abandon Izzie? Encourage you to carry on ignoring Luke? Is that your solution? Because if it is then we'd better say goodbye right now before we really start to hurt one another."

He grasped her arm. "That's not what I meant and you know it. I want to find a solution. I want to find a way to help all of us, but every time I try, you push me away. You won't marry me; you won't even move in with me. Maybe you think every man's dream is to grab at an occasional sexual adventure with a beautiful woman but it's not mine. I want you in my house and in my bed, and you're right…if you're not prepared to give me what I want, what I need, then we'll have to say goodbye. I thought I could wait…I even thought, given enough time, I could persuade you to change your mind…but this morning made me see how wrong I was. It doesn't matter what I do, what I say…you still put Luke first, and Izzie, and even your work at the riding school."

"Oh grow up Marcus! We're the adults here and the sooner you realize it the better." The words were out before she could stop them, spreading a bitterness between them that was almost tangible in the chill of the late afternoon. He stared at her for several seconds, and then he turned on his heel and walked away.

"Tell Luke I'm waiting in the car." He climbed into the driving seat, pulled the door shut behind him and switched on some music.

* * *

Jodie found Izzie and Luke brushing Buckmaster. With an effort she smiled at them. "Hello Luke. Bucky is really glad you decided to visit him. Would you like to give him a carrot?"

He shook his head. "Bucky eats hay, concentrates and supplements, not carrots. Supplements are prepared vitamin

175

or mineral pellets."

Jodie stared at him before turning in amazement to a grinning Izzie. "I guess you've been discussing horse feed today."

"Yep. I decided he needed something that was light relief from bird food, especially now he's moved onto worms and bugs thanks to poor old Blue."

Despite the feelings churning around inside her, Jodie smiled. "He needs to learn about treats too though. Horses like treats Luke, the same as you do. Here, give him a carrot now. He's been working hard today so he deserves it."

Luke ignored the carrot she held out to him. Instead he turned to Izzie. "Hay, concentrate and supplements," he repeated.

She laughed. "Yes, you're right Luke but I should have told you about the treats too. Bucky is allowed to have a carrot or an apple sometimes. Jodie is right. Everyone needs a treat occasionally."

The meaning behind her words was blatant but Jodie refused to bite. Instead she kept her voice neutral as she told Luke that Marcus was waiting for him in the car. Then she busied herself with Buckmaster's tack, first hanging his bridle on the hook provided and then carrying his saddle to the door.

"I'll take this over to the tack room," she told her sister. "You can take Luke to the car when he's finished with Bucky."

* * *

Jodie had been in the cottage long enough to start supper when Izzie finally joined her. Keeping her gaze fixed on the pan she was stirring she told her she was reheating some bolognaise sauce she'd found in the freezer and as it was almost ready she could lay the table. Without a word, Izzie did as she asked. She spoke as soon as they sat down though, her voice full of angry confusion.

"Why did you do it Jodie? Why did you send Marcus

away?"

"You're too young to understand…and anyway, I didn't send him away, he went all by himself. And we're not discussing it either. It's between Marcus and me. It's got nothing to do with you."

"But it has," Izzie's voice was a wail of protest. "How can you even think like that now Marcus and Luke are family? How can you throw something away that's good for all of us? How can you break Marcus' heart?"

"He'll survive," Jodie's voice was grim as she reached for the pepper. "He's an adult and that's what grownups do…they survive even if it means smashing their dreams."

"Like your dreams of being a champion dressage rider were smashed when you had to take care of me?"

"No, not like that at all. I chose to give up dressage because you were more important to me. I had a choice. Smashed dreams are the ones adults take a hammer to themselves."

"Like giving up on Marcus just because he isn't the sort of father you think he should be to Luke?"

Momentarily struck dumb by her sister's insight, Jodie stared at her. Then she shook her head. "It's more complicated than that. What we have…had…was precious…but it isn't strong enough to overcome our differences of opinion. How we feel about Luke will always come between us. So will the fact Marcus has so much money that he'll never understand why I need to keep working to stay independent."

"Well I think you're talking rubbish!" Izzie pushed away her plate and stood up so violently her chair tipped onto the floor behind her. "I've spent years wishing I had a family, years wanting someone else in our lives so you didn't have to do everything for me, and now you've found someone who loves you and I've found the closest thing to a younger brother I'm ever likely to have, you've taken it all away again. I hate you Jodie. I hate you for not telling me the truth about our mother. I hate you for being so uptight about everything all the time, and most of all I hate you for sending Marcus away."

Jodie watched as she stormed out of the room without a backward glance, then she pushed her own plate away and buried her face in her hands. Izzie was right. When she pushed Marcus into walking away she had only been thinking about herself, not what it would do to Izzie and Luke. She should have realized how deeply her sister felt about the man who had set her on the path to her dreams, and she should have realized, too, how much fun she had with Luke on the days when he wasn't locked into his own particular nightmares.

Well it was too late now. It was over, so they would just have to make the best of it. Izzie could carry on visiting the studio and if he could be persuaded, Luke could join the disabled riding program as planned. She would talk to Mrs. Cotton about it. Marcus didn't have to be involved anymore.

Dry-eyed she pushed herself away from the table and began to clear the dishes. When the last one was put away she went outside to check all the stables were secure and the gate was locked. After that she went to bed and stared at the window until the first streaks of dawn stretched across the sky.

\* \* \*

As the weeks went by things became slightly easier. During the day work took up most of Jodie's thinking time. Mrs. Cotton arranged for one of the younger care workers to bring Luke to the disabled riding program every Monday and Thursday. Izzie calmed down, and although she continued to spend most of her time at the studio, she never mentioned Marcus. By late summer life seemed the same as it had always been, except it wasn't. Beneath the casual conversations and hugs that were part and parcel of their lives, Jodie and Izzie were both aware of the rip in their relationship. Jodie knew, too, that there was one thing she still had to do. It ate away at her every time Izzie was in the house until in the end she couldn't bear it a moment longer.

"There's something else I haven't told you," she said

late one night while they were both getting ready for bed.

"If it's about Marcus, I don't want to know," the bitterness in her sister's voice made her wince.

"It's not. It's about the baby. You know, the one the monster was carrying in your nightmares."

"The baby the doctor cut out of our mother you mean. The one you didn't tell me about?"

"Yes. And I didn't tell you because I didn't realize you'd seen her. We've already been over that…what you don't know though…the other thing I haven't told you…is that she isn't dead. Somewhere in the world we have a sister but I don't know where she is."

With a sharp intake of breath Izzie sank down onto the side of her bed. "It didn't say she was alive in the newspaper article."

"I know. For some reason it didn't ever make the papers. I think most of the people who were there that night thought she had died, so the papers just concentrated on rehashing the highlights of Mamma's career. Somehow, though, the doctor who delivered her managed to keep her alive until she reached the hospital. She spent weeks in an incubator before she was fostered. Then she was put up for adoption. I was told there was no other choice because Mamma was dead. The authorities did manage to track Sean down but he refused to take responsibility for her, and I was considered far too young of course."

They stared at one another for a long moment and then they were in one another's arms, their tears mingling as they both started to speak.

"I'm sorry I was so horrible," Izzie got in first. "I don't hate you. I'll never hate you. I just wanted you and Marcus and Luke and me to be a family."

Jodie hugged her tightly. "I know, and I'm sorry it didn't work out. I'm sorry I didn't tell you about our sister either, but there didn't seem to be much point when I have absolutely no idea how to find her."

"I once asked the lawyer who set up your Trust Fund how I could contact her. He said because she was already with her new family it would be better for all of us if I forgot all about her and just concentrated on making a life for you and me. I know he meant well but it didn't make it any better. I wanted her…the same as I wanted you…and it hurt…it still hurts, the same as the way I abandoned you and Mamma hurts. If I'd stayed home with both of you instead of leaving the first chance I got, she would probably never have been on the motorway in the middle of the night, and you would never have been in that crash."

"You can't know that." Izzie pulled away slightly so she could look at her. "Nothing that happened is your fault Jodie. Marcus is right…you shouldn't keep blaming yourself for everything."

"Is there anything else you've discussed with Marcus I should know about?" Jodie's voice stiffened as she met her sister's gaze.

Izzie's cheeks flushed a defiant pink. "Only that he loves you."

"Which is one thing too many. I don't want you to talk to Marcus about me. Just concentrate on your music and leave me out of it."

# Chapter Twenty-eight

From then on things were easier. Jodie no longer had to worry about Izzie because following the final revelation about the dreadful car crash that had orphaned both of them, her sister's nightmares stopped completely. Within a matter of weeks Izzie changed from a gangly teenager with issues, into a much calmer and altogether more sophisticated young woman. Unlike Jodie, she didn't have to try to cope without Marcus and Luke either.

Although she appeared to have accepted they would never be a family she still saw both of them most days: working with Marcus at the studio and talking to Luke when he visited the riding school. She didn't socialize with them though. Nowadays she always came home to Jodie and there was a new thoughtfulness in the way she treated her. It was as if their final conversation about the baby had made her appreciate exactly what her sister had been through and now she considered it payback time. Jodie, however, had lived with her for too long to believe her attitude was entirely innocent.

After putting up with her sister's changed behavior for several weeks she finally cracked. Returning from her last lesson of the day to find a hot drink waiting for her and supper already on the table, she lowered herself into the nearest chair with scowl.

"Stop it! Just stop it! I know what you're trying to do but it's not going to work, so save yourself the effort. However much you try to soften me up I am not going to discuss Marcus with you, nor am I going to get back together with him, so whatever plan you've cooked up together, forget it. He and I are over and I'm moving on."

For the briefest moment Izzie tried to look hurt but then her expression hardened as she began to pile vegetables onto her plate. "If that's what moving on looks like then you'd be better to stay put. Have you looked at yourself in the mirror lately Jodie?"

Jodie had. She knew there were shadows beneath her eyes and she knew she had lost weight. She knew, too, that the frown line between her eyes hadn't been there before, the same way the pinched look around her mouth hadn't been there either. On the brief occasions she allowed herself to think about Marcus she wondered if he looked the same, or whether the Californian sunshine and the beautiful, leggy blonds that went with it, had helped him get over her. Wearily she shook her head.

"Leave it Izzie. I know what I'm doing so can we change the subject please. Tell me about your day."

\* \* \*

It was only later while she was settling Buckmaster for the night that she discovered she was crying. Mostly she stayed dry-eyed, the way she always had, but nowadays tears sometimes leaked out of her eyes without any warning. Angrily scrubbing them away she threw a blanket over the big chestnut horse. Then she buried her face in his flank and let the doubt that followed her around every minute of every day wash over her.

"I was too hard on him Bucky. I wanted him to change but I wasn't prepared to give him enough time. Why did I give up so soon? Why did I let my temper get the better of me? I should have had a bit more patience. If I had, then he might have learned to have faith in Luke?"

Buckmaster blew down his nose, a whoosh of sound that usually made her laugh. It didn't now though. Instead, it made her tears flow even faster as she realized that thanks to her own choices, it was soon going to be just her and Bucky, and that however much in tune with one another they were, he wasn't enough.

182

* * *

She woke the following morning with puffy eyes and a pounding headache. Anxious to escape from the house before Izzie saw her, she hurriedly pulled on the clothes she had worn the previous day and tiptoed down the stairs and out into the yard. Soon she was leading Buckmaster onto the lane leading to the bridleway.

As usual in the early morning, it was deserted, and she unlocked the gate and led Buckmaster through without any fear of being seen. Her dawn assignations with Marcus were a thing of the past, as were her visits to a house that nowadays was all but invisible thanks to the fast growing laurel hedge edging the driveway. She still kept her eyes averted though. She didn't want to see anything that reminded her of the good times.

Always in tune with her moods, Buckmaster plodded along. His ears were flat to his head and his normal joy de vivre was missing. He didn't give his usual whinny of delight when they topped the first sand dune and saw the sea either, nor did he kick up his heels when they reached the beach. Miserably Jodie leaned forward and patted him.

"You too Bucky?"

He dropped his head as she twitched the rein to direct him seawards and when they reached the ribbon of surf coming in on the tide, instead of high stepping into it and breaking into a gallop, he stood still.

Swallowing a sob Jodie pushed her feet into his flanks. "Come on Bucky. You've got to cheer up because there's nobody else on my side. Marcus has given up on us; Luke prefers to work with Carol instead of me; and Izzie's going to leave home soon…so please try, because I need all the support you can give."

He shook his head with a jingle of harness and then, as if he had understood every word she'd said, he responded to the pressure of her legs and set off up the beach as if he was being pursued by hornets.

183

* * *

Marcus watched them from where he was sitting at the top of the tallest sand dune, the same as he had watched them almost every morning since he'd last spoken to Jodie, He wondered how it had come to this. How had two people who had seemed so perfectly attuned to one another managed to get it so wrong? Was it because they had too much else to deal with, too much personal history to overcome, or was it just because they were both too stubborn to give in?

Much as he wanted to when they first split up, he knew he couldn't blame it on Luke. Jodie was right. He had spent years paying people to keep his son out of his hair. Instead of seeing him as someone with likes and dislikes and strengths and weaknesses, he hadn't even noticed he had any special skills until Jodie had shown him otherwise. It had always been easier to leave him to Mrs. Cotton and the rest of the care team and concentrate on his music.

His face burned with shame as he remembered how much he had resented Jodie's interest in Luke. What sort of father was he that he only wanted her for himself, not as part of a family unit? If he could accept Izzie without question why couldn't he accept his own son? Was it because he and Izzie had something in common and that he knew she would eventually fly the nest, whereas Luke probably wouldn't? He would always be around with his tantrums and obsessions, and the older he got the more difficult it was going to be, and yet Jodie had been prepared to face it and try to do something about it, so why couldn't he?

In the aftermath of their argument he had tried to find a solution but the mix of denial and despair that had been part of his life almost from the day Luke was born had gotten in the way. Frustrated and angry, he had finally decided to tackle it like a business problem, and embarked on a series of meetings with experts as well as visits to specialist schools, determined to find a way forward. Several times he had convinced himself he had, only to

184

wake up sweating in the middle of the night knowing it wasn't the answer he wanted. Mrs. Cotton and her team of care workers might not be the best solution, but whatever their shortcomings, surely they were better than sending his son away from home.

His reaction had startled him. Although he had always made sure Luke was well cared for he had never thought about how much he loved him. Well now he knew. He loved him the same way any other father loved his son, and because of that he had spent the past eleven years grieving for the person Luke would never be. And in all that time he had never once thought about the sort of person Luke could be given the right opportunities, whereas it was all that Jodie ever thought about.

It had taken him days to come to terms with how he felt, and more days to look at Luke's life as objectively as possible and accept how much he had let him down. From the outside Luke's twenty-four-hour care system made him look like a wonderful father, whereas now he could see it for the lie it was. He had neglected his son. Mrs. Cotton was used to Luke, and good with him, but she wasn't any sort of an expert. He should have brought a professional in to work with her years ago. She had started off as Luke's nanny and then, as he grew older, morphed into a sort of housekeeper-cum-team-leader. Thanks to her, every hour of his day was covered, but because she always followed Marcus' instructions to the letter, Luke's program hadn't altered in years. It was still the same one set up for him when it first became clear he couldn't cope with school. In the six years since, nothing had changed except his reading level and the complexity of his math.

Jodie was right. Luke deserved more. It wasn't enough for him to go to the gym or the swimming pool at the same time every day; neither were three hours of lessons every morning sufficient for a child with a brain as active as Luke's. He needed to find a way to give him more and the first step was to provide him with opportunities to leave the safety of his over-organized life. Maybe Jodie was right. Maybe the disabled riding program was the first step. Not that he had seen much progress so far but it was early days and anyway, what was the point of objecting when he didn't have any better ideas of his own.

He watched Jodie and Bucky grow smaller and smaller until they were a black dot in the distance and then he stood up and retraced his steps back to the house that was a prison, not just for Luke but for him too, because without Jodie it would never be a home.

* * *

By the time Jodie returned she was almost back to her normal self. The wind, the salt spray and the exercise had done much to restore her equanimity, and with a busy schedule waiting for her she had no time to brood. Leaving Buckmaster tucking in to the fresh hay she had forked into his feeding trough, she returned to the cottage. Izzie's curtains were still drawn so she was surprised to find her in the kitchen when she stepped inside.

"I thought you were still asleep," she said with a smile.

"I don't seem to be able to lie in like I used to. I guess it's because I'm sleeping better now the nightmares have gone." Izzie poured out a glass of orange juice as she spoke and pushed it across the table.

Jodie drank it gratefully and then tipped cereal and milk into a bowl and topped it with sliced banana.

Izzie tossed the discarded banana skin into the trashcan before she sat down opposite her. "I'm sorry about yesterday," she said. "I know I was out of line and I accept you don't want to talk about it but just tell me one thing will you? Do you love Marcus?"

For a moment Jodie stiffened but then all the fight went out of her. She nodded. "Yes…but I know it won't work. We have such differing views about Luke that we'd spend all our time arguing, plus Marcus gets really jealous if I spend too much time with him.

"What if I told you Marcus is really working at it? He's trying so hard Jodie. He's spent a fortune meeting with experts in the past few weeks. He even flew to the

186

States to visit a special school there to see if he could find a better solution for Luke's education."

Jodie shook her head. "It's not enough. Luke is a very bright little boy and I'm sure he could achieve a great deal with the right support but even the best education isn't the answer. What he needs is to know he's loved. He needs his Dad."

* * *

For the rest of the day Jodie took lessons, ordered feed, supervised the stable girls who were cleaning out the tack room, and was kept busy with the hundred and one other jobs that were part and parcel of running the riding school. All the time, however, she was aware that it was one of the days Luke came for his lesson and she wanted to talk to Carol before he arrived.

She had deliberately distanced herself from him after her argument with Marcus because she didn't want him confused by the fact she didn't visit him at home anymore. Sure it was better for him not to see her at all, she had asked Carol to supervise his lessons instead, and contented herself with a regular update on his progress.

Carol, who had her own theories about the shadows under Jodie's eyes and her increasingly short fuse, kept her thoughts to herself at their weekly meetings. Instead she did her best to put Luke in a good light even though she knew Jodie could see right through her. The truth was, he wasn't really benefiting at all. The most he had agreed to do so far was to stand at the side of the indoor arena with his care worker and watch the other riders walk around with the volunteer helpers. He wasn't always silent either. Sometimes the infernal clicking noises he made upset everyone around him, including the horses. Unhappy with what she was about to say, she poured Jodie a coffee, grabbed one for herself, and then settled into the chair opposite, using the pile of papers they had to go through as a barrier between them.

Anxious to put off the moment of truth, she began to

itemize them one by one as she slid them across the table to where Jodie sat, pen in hand. After half-a-dozen, however, she gave up.

"You don't want to do this now do you? You want to talk about Luke."

Taking Jodie's silence for acquiescence, she threw down her own pen, took a sip of her rapidly cooling coffee, and started to speak. Jodie didn't interrupt, nor did the expression on her face change, but when Carol finished she got up from the table, mug in hand, and walked across to the window. From there she could see everything in the yard, including Luke, who had just arrived.

He was wearing the old green baseball cap and fleece Izzie had given him and she knew it was because he associated it with her and with Izzie and Buckmaster. Whether she wanted to or not, it would be impossible for Mrs. Cotton to get him into jodhpurs and a proper riding hat. Only Izzie could do that. Or you could, the little voice in her head told her. Angrily she shook it away. She didn't want to listen to what she could or couldn't do for Luke, not when it was so painful.

"Shall I give it another go or should we call it quits?" Carol asked, coming to stand behind her. "After all we know it doesn't work for everyone. Maybe Luke is just resistant to horses."

Remembering how joyfully he had greeted Buckmaster in the days before Blue's death, Jodie took a deep breath. "Get one of the girls to saddle up Bucky please. Maybe he'll be better with a horse he knows."

Carol stared at her in horror. "For goodness sake Jodie whatever are you thinking of? I know Bucky is patient with the children...I know most of them love him...but he's far too big for a child as small as Luke. Don't forget he hasn't even agreed to sit on a pony yet, so he's not going to be thrilled when he sees a horse Buckmaster's size is he?"

Wishing she could shut out that maddening little voice that kept telling her she had to help Luke, Jodie turned away. "Ask his care worker if he'll wait a bit longer please. The arena will be empty in another fifteen minutes and that

188

might be all he needs, a space by himself."

With an unhappy shrug Carol hurried away to do her bidding. At least she'd tried so if it all went wrong it was on Jodie's head. Of course there was just a chance she was right. After all she was the one who'd taken the trouble to learn about children with autism, and she was the one who still went on training courses in her own time.

* * *

When Jodie led Buckmaster into the arena Luke was waiting for her. He looked very small standing beside Rob, his care worker, and when she led the big chestnut towards him he backed away.

"Hello Luke. Have you come to see Bucky today?"

When he didn't reply she carried on talking, keeping her words simple and factual with pauses in between to give him the time he needed to process them. Although he was super bright in some areas, she knew that stress frequently stopped him listening to the people who were talking to him, and today he was so stressed he wouldn't even look at her.

"I'm going to take Bucky for a walk Luke. Come with us. He likes you so he will like it if you walk with him."

As she spoke she started to lead Buckmaster around the arena. If he was watching her, Luke didn't show it. Instead he flapped his arms repetitively and began to click his tongue. Ignoring him, Jodie made a full circle of the indoor school before coming to a stop beside him again.

"Bucky liked that but he would like it better if you would come too Luke."

When he ignored her again, she repeated the circle. Then she did it a third and a fourth time. Finally, without looking at Luke, she left Buckmaster standing beside him and walked across to where some apples and carrots were stored in a plastic bin. Lifting the lid, she took out as many as she could hold and stuffed them into her pocket. Then she walked back to Buckmaster with her palm outstretched.

With a soft huff of pleasure, he gently scooped up the

189

windfall apple she had kept in her hand. She patted him and then smiled at Luke.

"That was his treat for walking so nicely. Would you like to give him a treat too Luke, just like you used to do?" She emptied the contents of her pocket onto the hay bale they sometimes used for mounting the horses, and waited.

It took a long time but eventually Luke moved away from his care worker and edged his way over to the heap of fruit and vegetables. Very carefully he separated them into two piles and then lined them up neatly. The young man who had brought him for his lesson rolled his eyes at Jodie, his patience near breaking point. She gave a slight smile as she shook her head. It was his job to look after Luke so he could stand there for however many hours it was going to take as far as she was concerned. Maybe he would even learn how to encourage Luke to achieve something new instead of just doing the same old thing every day.

Finally, after grading everything by size as well, Luke selected the smallest carrot and walked across to Buckmaster. Very slowly and deliberately he flattened his hand, balanced the carrot on it, and held it out. Holding her breath lest Bucky dislodge it and knock it to the ground in his eagerness to eat it, Jodie watched. Instead, to her utter amazement he took the carrot with unusual delicacy and then dipped his head so his ears were level with Luke's head.

\* \* \*

"It was a real obeisance," she told Izzie as they washed the dishes together at the end of their evening meal. "You know, the sort of respect he gives to me when he feels like it, but which he never, ever gives to anyone else."

"And what did Luke do?"

"He just gave him another carrot." Jodie laughed as she recalled Luke's actions at the end of the lesson. "He had no idea something special had happened. As far as he was concerned he was just feeding Bucky, and when there was no more food he started to make a fuss again."

190

"So what happens now?" Izzie finished drying the plate she was holding and placed it on top of the stack of dishes in front of her.

"He comes back tomorrow."

"That soon? I thought he was only booked in for a couple of lessons a week."

"He was, but even his care worker was impressed enough to agree it might be a good idea to bring him more frequently for a while."

"Is he always going to have lessons on his own or will you put him back in the class with the others?"

"A bit of both I think. That's if I can persuade him to sit on Buckmaster. It's early days yet but now Bucky is taking charge I'm really hopeful things will improve."

\* \* \*

She wasn't disappointed. In a matter of days Luke progressed from feeding Buckmaster carrots and apples to walking around the indoor arena holding onto his leading rein. He started talking again too. Not to her, but to the big chestnut horse who plodded along beside him. Jodie listened to his conversation with growing delight. He had remembered everything Izzie had told him about fodder and the correct diet for a horse, and he regaled it all to Buckmaster as they walked together. Eventually she joined in, gently correcting him when he got something wrong, and explaining how the exact quantities of food and water a horse needed depended on its size and how active it was.

By the time they moved onto the horse's digestive process he was hooked, and when she asked him if he wanted to help her to feed Buckmaster at the end of a lesson he was so excited he fairly danced across the yard to the stable.

Soon feeding Bucky was the highlight of his visit and eventually Jodie used it to get him up onto the horse's back. She started gently.

"You can take him back to his stable today," she told him as he rubbed his fingers across Bucky's velvety nose.

For a moment he looked doubtful.

"You can do it because it's almost the same as leading him around the arena and you've done that lots of times."

By the following day that, too, was part of his routine, and by now completely absorbed in the program she had put together for him. Jodie knew it was time to challenge him further. A few days later she did it by swinging herself up onto Buckmaster's back when the lesson finished.

"I'm going to ride Bucky back to his stable to feed him today Luke. You can see him again tomorrow."

She didn't look back as Buckmaster trotted out of the indoor school and across the yard, even though she could hear Luke complaining. Hardening her heart, she decided to leave his care worker to cope with him. It would do him good to have to think of a way to handle the change to Luke's routine, and now, after weeks of working with him, she knew he would be able to do it. He had stopped rolling his eyes and started to watch and listen to what she was saying weeks ago, and nowadays when he and Luke arrived for the lesson it was difficult to tell who was the most excited.

She sighed as she forked fresh hay into Buckmaster's stall. "Rob is only a kid himself Bucky; someone who is looking after Luke while he tries to discover what it is he really wants to do with his life. Why Marcus thought he was suitable I have no idea. Maybe it's because not many people want to spend day after day shut up with a challenging eleven-year-old, so he was all that was available. He's only doing it for the money anyway. He told me. He says when he's earned enough he's going travelling, so he's not really interested in what makes Luke tick."

Buckmaster gave her the long suffering look he always gave her when he wanted her to go away so he could eat his supper in peace. She chuckled as she slapped his rump. "It's alright, I'm going. You better prepare yourself though because tomorrow's the big day…I hope."

\* \* \*

192

When Luke arrived the following day it was clear he was angry with her. Rob shrugged when she raised a questioning eyebrow.

"He thinks you're feeding him too much hay."

She grinned at him. "Well if he thinks that then he had better learn to ride Bucky to his stable hadn't he…so he can feed him himself."

Luke stamped his way across to the bin and grabbed some apples and carrots. Jodie waited until he had laid them out in his usual orderly fashion before she said anything. Then, after making sure he was listening to her, she issued her challenge.

"How about it Luke? Can you sit on Bucky's back just like I do?"

When he ignored her, she swung herself up into the saddle and rode Buckmaster around the arena several times. Then she stopped beside him and slid off. Immediately Luke walked across to the hay bale and selected an apple but before he could hold it out, Jodie intercepted him.

"Not yet Luke. Bucky can't have a treat yet because he hasn't worked hard enough. He needs someone to ride him around the arena one more time before he can eat that apple."

After what seemed forever, Luke spoke to her. "You do it. You ride Bucky."

She shook her head. "I'm too tired to ride him again. It'll have to be someone else. I'll ask Rob to do it for me shall I?"

"NO!" Luke's roar of protest would have startled any other horse, but Buckmaster just blew down his nose and waited.

"Well if you don't want Rob to ride him, and I'm too tired, then you're going to have to do it yourself Luke."

Slowly he nodded. Then he walked across to the hay bale, moved the apples and carrots to one side and waited. Jodie gave an inward smile. So he had been taking everything in when he had just watched the other children have their lessons. He knew he had to stand on the hay bale to reach Bucky's back. He knew he had to hold onto the saddle pommel and put his left foot into the stirrup before he could swing his right leg over.

She watched him do it with a certain amount of trepidation and she didn't let go of him, even when he was sitting securely on Buckmaster's back. One small mistake and he could fall off and break his leg or worse.

"Don't let go of the saddle Luke, not until I've shortened the stirrups," she told him. "You need to be able to feel them with your feet before you can tell Bucky what you want him to do."

Out of the corner of her eye she saw Rob step forward, his face tense with anxiety. "Don't move," she hissed. "Don't do anything."

He stopped mid-stride and watched while she secured the stirrups and handed the reins to Luke. "Don't tug them," she instructed. "Bucky knows where he's going."

She kept one hand on his leg and held tightly onto the leading rein with the other as she led them both around the training arena. Then she gave Bucky an apple. Luke watched her approvingly and then he did as she asked and kicked his feet against Buckmaster's flanks. Immediately the horse started moving.

"Good boy Bucky," Jodie whispered as she led him out of the arena and across the yard. "Good boy."

# Chapter Twenty-nine

"God Jodie, you look absolutely exhausted. Go and have a bath. Use the oils I gave you for Christmas. A couple of drops of lavender or patchouli will help you relax."

Jodie gave a tired smile. "You listened then, when I used to add oils to your bath or put drops on your pillow to try to help you sleep?"

Izzie grinned at her. "I listened to everything you said, I just didn't let you know it. I must have been such an irritating child."

"No you weren't...well not often anyway. Maybe two or three times a day."

Her sister's peal of laughter followed her up the stairs, as did her promise to bring up a hot drink a little later. Going into the tiny bathroom that just fitted into the roof space, Jodie turned on both taps and then swirled a few drops of oil into the water. Within moments she was enveloped in fragrant steam and as she stripped off her clothes she felt herself begin to relax.

Lowering herself into the water she lay back and closed her eyes. Immediately images from the past week paraded across her eyelids: Luke climbing up onto Buckmaster's back; Luke letting her lead him around the arena; Luke laughing out loud the first time the big chestnut horse broke into a trot. With a groan she wondered what she was going to do about the growing bond between Bucky and the little boy.

From the outside it didn't appear to be that unusual. Many of the children on the riding program developed a special relationship with the horses they rode, but she knew Luke and Buckmaster had something different. Everything they did together had such a calming effect on Luke that, increasingly, he behaved like any other eleven-year-old boy when he was with the big chestnut gelding. It didn't matter whether he was sitting in the saddle, brushing Bucky's mane, or forking fresh hay into his food trough...everything he did made him happy. He was back to chattering non-stop too, although now his interests were all horse related.

Rob had noticed the improvement as well and had said things were also much better at home, adding a jokey afterthought. "Only as long as he knows he can come back tomorrow though, so don't ever take a day off will you Jodie?"

Sliding down under the water so her hair floated out around her in a billowing cloud, she wondered what she was going to do. The problem was she had been too successful with Luke and she knew she had done it by breaking every rule in the book. She had given him lessons at the same time every day; she hadn't involved any of the other instructors; she had let him spend all his time alone with Bucky instead of encouraging him to join a class; she had actually done everything she could to turn his riding lessons into a part of his daily routine. Had she done it because she wanted to help him or had she done it because she wanted to prove Marcus wrong, or had she done it for another reason entirely?

She surfaced in a swoosh of water and tipped shampoo into her hair, but all the time she was massaging her scalp and then sluicing away the soap with the shower head set on warm, a single thought kept going around in her head. Unless she could find a way to lessen Luke's reliance on her and Bucky then, whatever her original motivation had been, all she would have achieved was another problem for Marcus to deal with.

With a sigh she climbed out of the bath and wrapped herself in a towel. How could she have been so stupid, and what was Marcus going to do when he realized Luke had merely found another obsession, and that it involved the one person he didn't want to talk to any more?

It didn't take her long to find out because her cell phone rang while she was drying her hair. She scanned the caller ID, even though she knew it could only be one

196

person. Nobody else ever called her this late in the evening. For a moment she contemplated not answering but then her conscience about Luke got the better of her and she picked up.

"Jodie?" The sound of his voice after so long sucked the air from her lungs. Shakily she lowered herself onto the bed and cleared her throat.

"Hello Marcus."

"I need to speak to you about Luke and that horse of yours."

"I know...I'm sorry. It was a stupid thing to do. I'll find a way to sort it out, I promise...I..."

"Whatever are you talking about?" There was puzzlement in his voice as he interrupted her but she was too full of guilt to notice it.

"I...about Luke and Bucky...about making him too reliant on a daily routine at the riding school. I should have known better...I do know better...I don't know why I did it..."

There was a long pause and then he began to laugh. "So this is another of your failures is it? Another Jodie Eriksson fiasco where you've let everyone down."

Confused by his reaction she didn't answer. Instead she waited to hear what he would say next, wondering, as she did so, how she was going to be able to explain her actions. The silence between them went on for so long that for a moment she thought he'd cut the call. Then he spoke again only this time he wasn't laughing and there was a catch in his voice.

"I'm not calling to complain Jodie. I'm calling to thank you. I know Luke will always have problems so I was never expecting a cure but then I wasn't expecting a miracle either...and yet a miracle is what you've given me. Thanks to you and Bucky I now have a son who wants to tell me things. Each time he visits the stables he comes home and searches me out so we can talk about it. He tells me about Bucky and what they've done together. He tells me about the food he's given him. He tells me about you.

"What will it take to persuade you that everything

you've ever done in your life is close to a miracle Jodie? I've never met anyone who comes close to you for sheer bloody-mindedness. I don't think you know what the words 'giving up' mean, but I'm glad you are that way because otherwise you might have given up on Luke, like I did. What will it take to persuade you to forgive me for being such an obstinate idiot? What will it take to persuade you to trust me enough to marry me?"

The flush that had started in her cheeks suffused her whole body as his voice washed over her. In it she could hear a mix of love and doubt and fear as well as the memory of the bitter words they had spoken to one another the last time they met. She took a deep breath knowing there was only one way she could erase them.

"Maybe a lifetime together," she said.

\* \* \*

In the silence that followed she heard Izzie's footsteps on the stairs and turned towards the door; only when it opened it wasn't Izzie after all.

"Are you sure about that?" Marcus carried on speaking into his phone even though his eyes were locked on hers.

When she nodded he frowned. "Sorry, I can't hear you. The connection seems to be breaking up."

"I…I said…yes, I'll marry you." Jodie's answer was little more than a tremulous whisper as the sight of Marcus standing in the doorway threatened to overwhelm her, but it was enough. In a moment he had cut the call, tossed his cell phone onto the bed and she was in his arms.

\* \* \*

"I can't promise I'll never say or do stupid things again. I can't promise I'll never lose my temper; and sometimes, when I'm composing, you won't get a word out of me for days; but you'll always be able to trust me Jodie. I'm not your father, or your stepfather, or any of the rest of your mother's lovers…I won't leave you…I won't cheat on

198

you…and I'll do my very best to stay alive as well. All I'm ever going to do is love you." Marcus drew back slightly and tilted her face towards him.

She was serious as she looked up at him. "I know…I was just too frightened to accept it before. I've had to fight my own battles for so long that giving up some of my independence as well as the security of my job and the cottage seemed like such a big deal."

"So what changed your mind?"

Her sigh was heartfelt as she answered him. "I missed you."

He tightened his arms around her again. "Even after I was such an idiot?"

"Especially after you were such an idiot because that was when I got to see the real Marcus Lewis instead of Marcus Lewis the famous musician. Up until then I sometimes felt I was grasping at shadows. I would believe everything you told me for a while but then I'd lose faith again. I couldn't understand why you wanted someone like me in your life when you could take your pick of any one of a dozen beautiful women every time you went to California, or to anywhere else for that matter."

"You know that for sure do you?"

She buried her face in his sweater so her voice was muffled as she answered him. "It's difficult not to. I saw how everyone reacted when they heard you were moving here…and then there's Izzie. She told me almost everything there is to know about your career whether I wanted to hear it or not, especially about the days when you were touring."

"Let me guess…those would be the days when, according to the Press, all the girls in the audience threw their underwear at me, and I took a different groupie to bed every night?"

The top of her head brushed his chin as she nodded but he could hear the laughter beginning to bubble in her voice when she answered him. "That's right…except she didn't mention the groupie thing."

He chuckled. "Sensible girl. By the way she wants to

know if you're passing on the hot drink?"

With an effort Jodie twisted free of his arms and as she did so, the towel she had wrapped around herself finally unraveled and slithered slowly to the floor.

"What do you think?" she said

Epilogue

"I told you she was good," Marcus handed his companion a can of beer and then leaned on the railing fencing off the outdoor training arena and watched Jodie putting one of her pupils through his paces.

The man standing beside him nodded, his eyes fixed on the activity in front of him. "And yet you say she's not interested in publicity, let alone featuring in a documentary...or better still, a film. All the stuff she does here would make a terrific film if we sweetened it up a bit, threw in a love interest...you know the sort of thing."

"Yes, I do. And that's why she won't be interested. These kids can't be cured even though this sort of therapy does seem to help them in some indefinable way, so a film that tries to romanticize it would do more harm than good."

"Shame. A film like that. Just think of the box office. Your music, her story...children, animals; it couldn't fail."

"Maybe, but it's something you're never going to know...now have you seen enough? Are you ready to do what you actually came for, and talk about Izzie's next release?"

Marcus' agent grinned as he finished his beer and crushed the can. "Okay I know when I'm beaten. Is she in the studio already?"

"No. See the girl in the bright pink beanie leading the child on the small pony...that's Izzie. She says she's just keeping her hand in but, truth be told, I think she misses the countryside when she's away on tour. The first thing she does whenever she comes home is to change into her jodhpurs and go riding with Luke."

The older man shook his head. "And you won't even let me take a promotional shot of that will you, despite the fact it would help sell thousands more of her songs? Bella Blue on a horse, riding bareback, with those long, long legs dangling. Just think how fantastic it would look. Come on Marcus, you know it would be an absolute winner."

"Not a chance. And don't try to get there through Izzie either because she isn't Bella Blue when she's here, she's just Izzie, and she values every minute of her privacy. She's very protective of Luke too, and Jodie, so she would never countenance anything that would push them into the limelight."

Okay! Okay! I know when I'm beaten, even though I think you should be shouting from the rooftops about the work that's going on here. Think of all the accolades you would get if the public knew how much money you pour into this therapy centre."

"For what...just so I can feel good about myself. You know me better than that. If I sold out on Jodie and her principals, and on Luke, then all I'd have left would be a sour taste in my mouth and a very angry wife."

"I guess, but she's one lucky lady to have you at her back."

Marcus shook his head. "You don't know the half of it. I'm the lucky one here, and I aim to keep it that way."

* * *

Their meal over, and confident Izzie and Luke would remain on the couch in the family room for the next hour or so while they watched a film and ate popcorn, Marcus and Jodie slipped into the adjoining sitting room with conspiratorial smiles.

"Why do I feel like I'm doing something wrong in my own house," Marcus whispered as he sank down into a recliner and pulled her onto his lap.

She grinned at him. "Because this is how it all started, remember?"

"You mean that weekend in London when all you would let me do was snatch a few moments with you when Izzie and Luke weren't looking?"

"Mmm…and I refused to come to your bedroom even though I was sure it was the only reason you'd invited us to stay with you."

"It was not! It was so we could get to know one another better." Even to Marcus' ears, his protest had a hollow ring, and soon they were laughing at the memory. As always though, it was laughter that quickly settled into something else as their lips touched and their bodies ignited into a familiar passion.

Eventually, with a groan of frustration, Marcus settled her more comfortably on his lap. "Unless you want me to disgrace myself right here, just lie still."

Searching for somewhere to rest her head she found it in the angle between his arm and his shoulder and relaxed into it with a sigh. "You started it."

"So I did but that was before I remembered how long it's going to be until Luke and Izzie go to bed."

* * *

Much later, when all the windows were in darkness, they walked together across the garden to the horse therapy centre that stood next to Marcus' studio, and which was now such an integral part of their home. The scatters of stars were pinpoints in the midnight blue of the sky, and for one brief moment the silence was absolute. Then it was broken by familiar night sounds: the occasional complaint of a roosting bird; the rush of wings as an owl flew overhead; the snorts and grunts of resting horses. Listening to the rustle of straw, the occasional whinny, the sound of a heavy body accidentally knocking against a stable door, Jodie gave a sigh of contentment.

Marcus smiled down at her. "This is where your heart truly belongs, isn't it?"

"Only if you're here too."

"Well I'm not going anywhere…not even to California in the foreseeable future. Writing songs and musical arrangements for Izzie's next tour is taking up all of my time these days."

Jodie didn't answer until she had checked all the horses and given Buckmaster one last pat on the long blaze of white on his forehead. Then, with the doors to each stable securely locked behind her, she turned back to Marcus, slipped her arms around his neck and raised herself up on tiptoe so she could kiss him.

"Thank you."

"For what? For bullying you into marrying me?"

She laughed. "Yes…and for helping Izzie to realize her dream…and for forgiving me for having such a bad temper…and for making me see there's nothing wrong with giving up a little bit of independence if you love someone…but most of all, for this. You've helped me do something I didn't even know I wanted to do before I met Luke. To be able to concentrate on horse therapy full time without having to worry about livery charges and riding lessons and all those other things that kept the riding school afloat…it's a dream come true. I wake up every morning and pinch myself to check it's real."

He returned her kiss with force. "And here I was hoping it was all about me."

"It is! It is! You know it is Marcus…always and forever." Then her laughing protestations were lost as his arms tightened around her again until they became a single black shadow against the bright backdrop of the moon; and soon their own sighs were added to the small sounds of the night.

The End

**Also from Books We Love by Sheila Claydon**

Cabin Fever
Double Fault
Reluctant Date
Kissing Maggie Silver
Sheila Claydon Special Edition
Finding Bella Blue (When Paths Meet  Book 2)
Saving Katy Gray (When Paths Meet Book 3)
Miss Locatelli
Remembering Rose (Mapleby Memories Book 1)

Sheila Claydon agrees with the late Ray Bradbury: *'First, find out what your hero wants. Then just follow him.'* She starts with plots, chapter outlines and characters; she knows all the rules and faithfully follows them each time she starts to write a new story. Then the hero takes over and she follows him instead.

She can be contacted on http://sheilaclaydon.com where her books are listed, and where she also writes an occasional blog. Also at facebook.com/SheilaClaydon.author and on twitter

bookswelove.com